Henry Wadsworth Longfellow, Harry Arbuthnot Acworth

**Scenes From The saga of King Olaf**

Op.30

Henry Wadsworth Longfellow, Harry Arbuthnot Acworth

**Scenes From The saga of King Olaf**
*Op.30*

ISBN/EAN: 9783744783460

Printed in Europe, USA, Canada, Australia, Japan

Cover: Foto ©Andreas Hilbeck / pixelio.de

More available books at **www.hansebooks.com**

NOVELLO'S ORIGINAL OCTAVO EDITION.

COMPOSED FOR THE NORTH STAFFORDSHIRE MUSICAL FESTIVAL, OCTOBER, 1896.

SCENES FROM THE SAGA OF

# KING OLAF

BY

### H. W. LONGFELLOW

AND

### H. A. ACWORTH, C.I.E.

SET TO MUSIC

FOR SOPRANO, TENOR, AND BASS SOLI, CHORUS, AND ORCHESTRA

BY

# EDWARD ELGAR

(OP. 30).

(PRICE FOUR SHILLINGS AND SIXPENCE.).

Paper boards, 5s. 6d. ; cloth, 7s. 6d.

LONDON : NOVELLO AND COMPANY, LIMITED.

NEW YORK : THE H. W. GRAY CO., SOLE AGENTS FOR THE U.S.A.

# KING OLAF.

## INTRODUCTION.

### SOLI and CHORUS.

There is a wondrous book
Of Legends in the old Norse tongue,
Of the dead kings of Norroway,—
Legends that once were told or sung
In many a smoky fireside nook
Of Iceland, in the ancient day,
By wandering Saga-man or Scald;
Heimskringla is the volume called;
And he who looks may find therein
The story that we now begin.

---

### No. 1.—RECIT. (Bass).

*Summon now the God of Thunder,*
*Him who rives the heav'ns asunder,*
*Sing the words of mighty Thor*
*Challenging the world to war.*

## CHALLENGE OF THOR.

### No. 2.—CHORUS.

I am the God Thor,
I am the War God,
I am the Thunderer!
Here in my Northland,
My fastness and fortress,
Reign I for ever!

Here amid icebergs
Rule I the nations;
This is my hammer,
Miölner the mighty;
Giants and sorcerers
Cannot withstand it!

There are the gauntlets
Wherewith I wield it,
And hurl it afar off;
This is my girdle;
Whenever I brace it,
Strength is redoubled!

The light thou beholdest
Stream through the heavens
In flashes of crimson,
Is but my red beard
Blown by the night-wind,
Affrighting the nations!

Jove is my brother;
Mine eyes are the lightning;
The wheels of my chariot
Roll in the thunder.
The blows of my hammer
Ring in the earthquake!

Force rules the world still,
Has ruled it, shall rule it;
Meekness is weakness,
Strength is triumphant.
Over the whole earth
Still is it Thor's-Day.
Thou art a God too,
O Galilean!
And thus single-handed
Unto the combat,
Gauntlet or Gospel,
Here I defy thee!

*(Longfellow.)*

## KING OLAF'S RETURN.

### No. 3.—SOLO (Tenor).

And King Olaf heard the cry,
Saw the red light in the sky,
    Laid his hand upon his sword,
As he leaned upon the railing,
And his ship went sailing, sailing
    Northward into Drontheim fiord.

There he stood as one who dreamed;
And the red light glanced and gleamed
    On the armour that he wore;
And he shouted, as the rifted
Streamers o'er him shook and shifted,
    "I accept thy challenge, Thor!"

To avenge his father slain,
And reconquer realm and reign,
    Came the youthful Olaf home,
Through the midnight sailing, sailing,
Listening to the wild wind's wailing,
    And the dashing of the foam.

To his thoughts the sacred name
Of his mother Astrid came,
    And the tale she oft had told
Of her flight by secret passes
Through the mountains and morasses,
    To the home of Hakon old.

Then strange memories crowded back
Of Queen Gunhild's wrath and wrack,
    And a hurried flight by sea;
Of grim Vikings, and their rapture
In the sea-fight, and the capture,
    And the life of slavery.

Then his cruisings o'er the seas,
Westward to the Hebrides,
    And to Scilly's rocky shore;
And the hermit's cavern dismal,
Christ's great Name and rites baptismal,
    In the ocean's rush and roar.

Norway never yet had seen
One so beautiful of mien,
    One so royal in attire,
When in arms completely furnished,
Harness gold-inlaid and burnished,
    Mantle like a flame of fire.

\*    \*    \*    \*    \*    \*

Thus came Olaf to his own,
When upon the night-wind blown
    Passed that cry along the shore:
And he answered, while the rifted
Streamers o'er him shook and shifted,
    "I accept thy challenge, Thor!"
                    (*Longfellow*.)

---

No. 4.—RECIT. (*Bass*).

*Tell how Olaf bore the Cross
To the folk at Nidaros,
Norland, Iceland, lands and seas
Winning to the God of Peace.*

## THE CONVERSION.

No. 5.—SCENE (*Tenor and Bass Soli
and Chorus*).

*Chorus.*

King Olaf's prows at Nidaros
    Furrowed the golden shore,
His axemen and his bowmen
    Lay round the shrine of Thor.

Round the stately fane at Mærin
    King Olaf's housecarles lay,
And watch'd the men of Drontheim
    Gather at break of day.

Mail-clad they came, and sworded,
    Corslet and buckler ring
As they throng behind the Ironbeard
    Who leads them to the King.

The shipmen grave of Iceland
    Retir'd to give them room,
Their ringèd mail was rusted
    And gray with salt-sea spume.

All halted, all were silent,
    When, shiv'ring through the blue,
Smiting the walls of Asgard,
    King Olaf's bugle blew.

### OLAF (*Tenor*).

Behold me, my people, and answer and say
If the gods of your fathers ye worship to-day?
Or bend ye your will to the word of your King,
To the waters of Christ and the Cross that I
    bring?

### IRONBEARD (*Bass*).

By my beard called of iron, O King, thou shalt
    know
In the name of thy people, I answer thee, "No."

Shall thy cross and thy waters purge out the
    gods' ban,
Who feed on the flesh and the life-blood of man?

### OLAF.

Shall Thor and shall Odin be high gods agen?
Then give to their altars their guerdon of iren.

But shall blood of base losels and felons restore
The glow to the altars of Odin and Thor?

Nay, a sacrifice rich to their shrines will I yield,
My fairest in bower and best under shield.

My mightiest dies there, by sun and by moon,
Ironbeard, and my fairest, his daughter Gudrun.

### IRONBEARD.

Not the fair or the mighty, Gudrun or her sire,
Shall pass by thy mandate, O King, through
    the fire.

See above in the sun gleams the image of gold,
Of Thor with the battle-maul gripp'd in his hold;

If he seeks for a hero, his hest thou shalt do,
Call the best of thine axemen and offer thereto.

### OLAF.

O hearken, my people, behold me once more,
And may Christ lift my axe 'gainst the hammer
    of Thor.

*Chorus.*

As leap the lights of winter
    Athwart the northern sky,
Against the golden image
    Flash'd Olaf's axe on high.

As falls a berg in springtime,
  Far shiver'd on the floe,
The golden shards of godhead
  Crash'd on the ground below.

Fierce Ironbeard sprang forward ;
  A housecarle drew his bow,
And o'er the shattered image
  Its champion lay low.

IRONBEARD.

All-Father, I come ! true to honour and troth,
To the faith of my fathers, and Odin the Goth.

O wide should the doors of Valhalla unroll
For a hero who gives for it body and soul.

King Olaf the Norseman ! perchance it shall be,
That thy Peace-God may rule o'er the
    Norlander free ;

But with axe in his hand, and with sword upon
    thigh,
And his face to his slayer doth Ironbeard die.

*Chorus.*

Then o'er the blood-stained Horg-stone
  The Cross of Christ was seen,
The holy priests were praying,
  The singers sang between.

King Olaf's axe was lower'd,
  His bright blue eyes were dim,
As swung the golden censer,
  As swelled the solemn hymn.

The men of Drontheim trembled,
  They marvell'd and they knelt ;
Their helpless god was broken,
  The power of Christ was felt.

OLAF.

O brothers of Iceland, behold them, they kneel !
Of my Lord and His conquest, come, be you
    the seal.

Pass the gods of the Gothland ; your serfdom
    shall cease,
For the sacrifice bloody I offer you peace :
The peace of the Christian ; O, join in the
    prayer
That swells to the Lord of the earth and the
    air.

*Chorus.*

Receive us, King ; we kneel to Him
Who felled by thee the War-god grim ;

Water bring, our brows to lave,
On our shields the Cross engrave ;

Blood and battle let them cease,
Knit us to the God of peace.

OLAF (*with Chorus*).

Lord, receive them ! King divine,
Breathe a blessing ; they are Thine.
                        (*Acworth.*)

---

No. 6.—RECIT. (*Bass*).

*Now the child of Ironbeard dead,*
*Fair Gudrun, doth Olaf wed,*
*Hoping thus, his wergild paying,*
*To redeem him from the slaying.*

## GUDRUN.

No. 7.—SCENE (*Soprano and Tenor Soli*
          *and Chorus*).

*Soprano.*

On King Olaf's bridal night
Shines the moon with tender light,
And across the chamber streams
    Its tide of dreams.

At the fatal midnight hour,
When all evil things have power,
In the glimmer of the moon
    Stands Gudrun.

Close against her heaving breast,
Something in her hand is pressed ;
Like an icicle, its sheen
    Is cold and keen.

On the cairn are fixed her eyes
Where her murdered father lies,
And a voice remote and drear
    She seems to hear.

*Chorus.*

What a bridal night is this !
Cold will be the dagger's kiss ;
Laden with the chill of death
    Is its breath.

Like the drifting snow she sweeps
To the couch where Olaf sleeps ;
Suddenly he wakes and stirs,
    His eyes meet hers.

OLAF (*Tenor*).

" What is that," [King Olaf said],
" Gleams so bright above thy head?
   Wherefore standest thou so white
      In pale moonlight?"

GUDRUN (*Soprano*).

" 'Tis the bodkin that I wear
When at night I bind my hair;
   It woke me falling on the floor;
      'Tis nothing more."

OLAF.

Forests have ears, and fields have eyes;
Often treachery lurking lies
   Underneath the fairest hair!
      Gudrun, beware!"

*Chorus.*

Ere the earliest peep of morn
Blew King Olaf's bugle horn;
   And for ever sundered ride
      Bridegroom and bride!
         (*Longfellow.*)

---

No. 8.—RECIT. (*Bass*).

*How the Wraith of Odin old*
*Song and tale and Saga told,*
*Coming as unbidden guest*
*To the hall, to Olaf's feast;*
*Sing ye now, and with the strain*
*Ancient memories wake again.*

# THE WRAITH OF ODIN.

## No. 9.—CHORUS (BALLAD).

The guests were loud, the ale was strong,
King Olaf feasted late and long;
The hoary Scalds together sang;
O'erhead the smoky rafters rang.
   (Dead rides Sir Morten of Fogelsang.)

The door swung wide, with creak and din;
A blast of cold night-air came in,
And on the threshold shivering stood
A one-eyed guest, with cloak and hood.
   (Dead rides Sir Morten of Fogelsang.)

The King exclaimed, " O graybeard pale!
Come warm thee with this cup of ale."
The foaming draught the old man quaffed,
The noisy guests looked on and laughed.
   (Dead rides Sir Morten of Fogelsang.)

Then spake the King : " Be not afraid;
Sit here by me." The guest obeyed,
And seated at the table, told
Tales of the sea, and Sagas old.
   (Dead rides Sir Morten of Fogelsang.)

As one who from a volume reads,
He spake of heroes and their deeds,
Of lands and cities he had seen,
And stormy gulfs that tossed between.
   (Dead rides Sir Morten of Fogelsang.)

Then from his lips the music rolled
The Havamal of Odin old,
With sounds mysterious as the roar
Of billows on a distant shore.

\*     \*     \*     \*     \*     \*

Then slept the King, and when he woke
The guest was gone, the morning broke.
   (Dead rides Sir Morten of Fogelsang.)

They found the doors securely barred,
They found the watch-dog in the yard,
There was no foot-print in the grass,
And none had seen the stranger pass.
   (Dead rides Sir Morten of Fogelsang.)

King Olaf crossed himself and said :
" I know that Odin the Great is dead;
Sure is the triumph of our Faith,
The one-eyed stranger was his Wraith!"
   (Dead rides Sir Morten of Fogelsang.)
      (*Longfellow.*)

---

No. 10.—RECIT. (*Bass*).

*Sisters, sing us now the song*
*How since Olaf came a-wooing,*
*Sigrid wrought for his undoing,*
   *Of the insult and the wrong.*

# SIGRID.

No. 11.—SCENE (*Soprano and Tenor Soli*
   *and Chorus of Maidens*).

*Chorus.*

Sigrid sits in her high abode,
The haughty Queen of Svithiod,
   And to the West looks she
For Norroway's King whose suit is told
By the ring from Ladè's temple old,
   Which lies upon her knee.

Lady, lady, lances gleam
On the farther side of the border stream;
Lady, the horses ford the flood,
They cross the meadow, and pass the wood,

You may hear the iron hoof-stroke beat
On the ringing stones of the village street;
Rank on rank came spearmen tall,
But the crest of Olaf is o'er them all,
    And the peace strings bind his sword;
See, he alights, he mounts the stair,
The Norroway King with the golden hair,
    Queen Sigrid, greet thy lord.

### OLAF (Tenor).

Sigrid, hail! with royal hand
Knit to thee Norroway's King and land,
And the ring of Ladè upon thy knee
We will change to a cross for thee and me.

### SIGRID (Soprano).

Olaf, hail! my hand is thine,
But the gods of old I will not resign;
Bow thou to thy Cross for woe or weal,
But where I have knelt, I still must kneel.

### OLAF.

Queen of Svithiod! hearken well,
Thy gods are mute on fiord and fell,
Nor ever shall their voice again
Be heard where Christ hath ris'n to reign.

### SIGRID.

I hear them speak! from pole to pole
The Norland gods their thunder roll;
For Norland folk their sword—the rod
For slaves who own the Southland god.

### OLAF.

I will give my body and soul to flame
Ere I take to my heart a heathen dame;
Thou hast not beauty, thou hast not youth,
Shall I buy thy land at the cost of truth?

### Chorus.

King Olaf rises; sisters, say
Why does he thrust the Queen away,
Why dash his glove on the oaken floor,
And turn and stride towards the door?
The gods protect the wrong'd and weak!
The glove has struck Queen Sigrid's cheek,
See the flash of her haughty eye,
See her stately form drawn high!
Haste thee, O haste, King Olaf, fly.

### SIGRID.

Thou art gone! nay, spur not through the
    gate;
I am one that can watch and wait;

By yonder glove on the oaken floor,
By my father's head and the soul of Thor,
By the hand she offered, Sigrid saith,
That Sigrid yet shall be Olaf's death.
             (*Acworth.*)

---

### No. 12.—RECIT. (*Bass*).

*Hark! she flies from Wendland forth,*
*Slighted Thyri, to the North:*
*There, as Olaf's wedded dame,*
*Will she set the North aflame!*

# THYRI.

### No. 13.—CHORUS (BALLAD).

A little bird in the air
Is singing of Thyri the fair,
    The sister of Svend the Dane:
And the song of the garrulous bird
In the streets of the town is heard
    And repeated again and again.
      (Hoist up your sails of silk,
      And flee away from each other.)

To King Burislaf, it is said,
Was the beautiful Thyri wed,
    And a sorrowful bride went she:
And after a week and a day,
She has fled away and away,
    From his town by the stormy sea,
      (Hoist up your sails of silk,
      And flee away from each other.)

They say, that through heat and through
    cold,
Through weald, they say, and through wold,
    By day and by night, they say,
She has fled: and the gossips report
She has come to King Olaf's court,
    And the town is all in dismay.
      (Hoist up your sails of silk,
      And flee away from each other.)

It is whispered King Olaf has seen,
Has talked with the beautiful Queen;
    And they wonder how it will end;
For surely, if here she remain.
It is war with King Svend the Dane,
    And King Burislaf the Vend!
      (Hoist up your sails of silk,
      And flee away from each other.)

O, greatest wonder of all!
It is published in hamlet and hall.
    It roars like a flame that is fanned
The King—yes, Olaf the King—

Has wedded her with his ring,
  And Thyri is Queen in the land !
    (Hoist up your sails of silk,
    And flee away from each other.)
               (*Longfellow.*)

### No. 14.—DUET (*Soprano and Tenor*).

#### THYRI.

The gray land breaks to lively green,
  Bespangled all with flowers;
The throstles sing to greet the spring
  Through lengthening sunlit hours.

But what care I for flowers on sward,
  Or bursting buds on tree?
My lands restored from Wendland's lord
  Were better cheer to me.

A landless, dowerless bride am I,
  The bride of Norroway's King,
What boots me, while I sit and sigh,
  The coming of the spring?

#### OLAF.

Thyri, my beloved,
  Hither come I bearing
Angelicas uprooted,
  Sweet and fair as thou.
Earliest boon of springtime,
Sign of snow departing,
In their welcome fragrance,
  Bathe thy snowy brow.

#### THYRI.

Sweet are thy words, but O ! meseems,
  A sweeter gift would be,
The boon that haunts Queen Thyri's
    dreams,
  Her dowry over sea.
Wide spread they from the Wendland shore,
  And rich with fruit and flower,
The lands I weep for evermore,
  O ! give me back my dower.

#### OLAF.

Fear not, doubt not, weep not,
  As a Queen triumphant,
Towards the happy sunlight
  Lift thy radiant eyes;
To the strife of favours,
For thy love I gird me,
And the lands of Thyri
  Shall I win for prize.

#### BOTH.

Comes the spring unchaining,
Sunshine on his pinions,
All the world imprisoned
  In the Ice-King's hall;
So the golden promise
Passed from lord to lady,
Warm with words of loving,
  Lifts the heart from thrall.
            (*Acworth.*)

### No. 15.—CHORAL RECIT.

*After Queen Gunhild's death,*
*So the old Saga saith,*
*Plighted King Svend his faith,*
  *To Sigrid the Haughty.*

*Still on her scornful face,*
*Blushing with deep disgrace,*
*Bore she the crimson trace*
  *Of Olaf's gauntlet.*

*Oft to King Svend she spake,*
*" For thine own honour's sake*
*Shalt thou swift vengeance take*
  *On this vile coward ! "*

*And to avenge his bride,*
*Soothing her wounded pride,*
*Over the waters wide*
  *King Olaf sought he.*
           (*Longfellow.*)

## THE DEATH OF OLAF.

### No. 16.—CHORUS.

King Olaf's dragons take the sea,
The piping south-wind drives them fast,
The shields dip deep upon the lee,
The white sails strain on every mast.
Leaping from wave to wave they round
The cape that bars the stormy sound,
And where the ocean opens wide
They see far stretched on either side
The Danish ships and Svithiod's ride;
High on his deck King Olaf stands,
The war-axe grasp'd in both his hands,
With helm of gold and jerkin red,
And fair curls blowing round his head,
First of his fleet, he leads the van
And seeks the battle, man to man.

But seaward, landward, cape and bay
Cast forth their foes on Norroway;
Ten thousand shaven oar-blades sweep
The bosom of the troubled deep;

As crash the prows, ring bill and shield,
And arm meets arm that will not yield;
Still where the foemen thickest throng
King Olaf's galley sweeps along,
And still her lofty sides to scale
Ply the fierce foemen oar and sail,
And pour their heroes bright in mail,
    Woe, woe for Norroway!
O'erwhelmed, her stout sea-dragons fly,
Or, scatter'd, powerless, scarcely try
    To join once more the fray:

Yet still, like sunbeam through a cloud,
Glimmers the helm of Olaf proud,
    Faint and more faint to see:
Around it close the dark'ning spears,
It sinks, it sparkles, disappears,
    King Olaf, woe to thee!

Thy latest fight is fought in vain,
No more the axe of Olaf slain,
    No more the glittering crest,
Shall victory pluck from ruin's verge,
Or to the chase his spearmen urge;
Above him rolls the sullen surge,
    That stormy heart has rest.
              (*Acworth.*)

---

## EPILOGUE.

### SOLI AND CHORUS.

#### *Bass Recit.*

*In the convent of Drontheim*
*Knelt Astrid, the Abbess,*
*At midnight, adoring.*
*She heard in the silence*
*The voice of one speaking*
*Without in the darkness,*
*Now louder, now nearer,*
*Now lost in the distance.*

#### *Soli and Chorus.*

"It is accepted,
  The angry defiance,
  The challenge of battle!

It is accepted,
But not with the weapons
Of war that thou wieldest!

"Cross against corslet,
Love against hatred,
Peace-cry for war-cry!
Patience is powerful;
He that o'ercometh
Hath power o'er the nations!

#### *Chorus (unaccompanied).*

"As torrents in summer,
Half-dried in their channels.
Suddenly rise, though the
Sky is still cloudless,
For rain has been falling
Far off at their fountains;

"So hearts that are fainting
Grow full to o'erflowing,
And they that behold it
Marvel, and know not
That God at their fountains
Far off has been raining!

#### *Soli and Chorus.*

"Stronger than steel
Is the sword of the Spirit;
Swifter than arrows
The light of the truth is,
Greater than anger
Is love, and subdueth!

"The dawn is not distant,
Nor is the night starless,
Love is eternal!
God is still God, and
His faith shall not fail us;
Christ is eternal!"

---

A strain of music ends the tale,
A low, monotonous, funeral wail,
That with its cadence, wild and sweet,
Makes the long Saga more complete.
            (*Longfellow.*)

---

NOTE.—In the following Scenes it is intended that the performers should be looked upon as a gathering of skalds (bards); all, in turn, take part in the narration of the Saga and occasionally, at the more dramatic points, personify for the moment some important character.

    The names of persons and places should be pronounced generally as in German.

              E. E.

# SYNOPSIS.

## INTRODUCTION.

The bards name and describe the book in which is written the story they are about to relate.

*One of their number, who is evidently recognised to be the chief bard or master of the ceremonies, calls upon the members of the company to constitute themselves as representing Thor, the God of thunder, and to repeat his challenge.*

## THE CHALLENGE OF THOR.

The whole assembly, in response to its chief, is here supposed to represent Thor, who arrogates to himself supremacy in the world, and hurling out defiance to the Christian religion, issues a challenge to Christ its prototype.

## KING OLAF'S RETURN.

Another of the bards comes forward and relates how the fugitive Olaf hears and accepts the challenge, and after recounting the youthful Olaf's wanderings and adventures previous to that time, tells of his return home to Norway as King, and of his resolve to establish Christianity in the kingdom.

*Their chief here directs the Skalds to tell how Olaf accomplished his mission.*

## THE CONVERSION.

In this scene, the minstrels describe the gathering of Olaf's subjects at the temple of their deity; headed by Ironbeard, they meet the king and his bodyguard of axemen and bowmen.

King Olaf, in the person of the tenor bard, offers the religion of Christ to the people, and Ironbeard—which character is for the nonce assumed by the chief bard—in the name of the people refuses it; whereupon the king, goaded to the act by the defiant words and attitude of Ironbeard, takes up his war-axe and shatters the image of Thor. In attempting to avert the destruction of the idol, Ironbeard is mortally wounded, but, defiant to the last, the grim old warrior declares himself staunch to the faith of his fathers. With dying breath he commends his soul to Odin (the chief god of the Norse religion), and claiming entrance into Walhalla, the eternal paradise of heroes slain in battle, expires.

The people are so much impressed by the manifestation of Thor's impotence and the death of his champion, that they elect to embrace the new faith, the peace of which, and its completed sacrifice, the king offers them as an alternative to the ever-recurring sacrifices of blood demanded by the tenets of their religion. Meekly surrendering themselves to the newly-revealed power, in solemn unity they bow before their king, who, with thrilling intensity, invokes upon his kneeling subjects the blessing of the King divine.

*The master bard himself tells how, as a blood-atonement, Olaf weds Gudrun, the daughter of Ironbeard.*

## GUDRUN.

The company of Skalds describes how Gudrun, intent on avenging her father's death, steals, on the bridal night, with dagger in hand, to where Olaf sleeps; but Olaf wakes and thwarts her design, and ere the dawn of morn rids himself of the treacherous bride.

*The chief minstrel now commands his men to sing of the coming, as an unbidden guest to Olaf's feast, of the spirit of Odin.*

## THE WRAITH OF ODIN.

In the words of a stirring ballad, the assembled bards sing of the strange guest who entertained the company far into the night with his wonderful stories. How the king slept, but woke to find the guest gone; how Olaf, finding no trace of the departure of the stranger, pronounced him to have been the spirit of Odin, and interpreted the visitation to signify the downfall of Odin the Great, and the effectual triumph of the Christian faith.

*The chief bard invites the maidens of the company to sing the story of the wooing of Queen Sigrid by King Olaf, of the insult she suffered at his hands, and of her vow to accomplish his death.*

## SIGRID.

The minstrel maids sing of the Queen of Svithiod awaiting the coming of King Olaf, with the ring, taken by Olaf from Lade's temple, on her knee.—The two characters are again represented by bards.

# SYNOPSIS (*continued*).

Olaf arrives, greets the queen, and offers her himself, his land, and his religion.

Sigrid returns the greeting, but will only consent to become his, on condition he swears his love, as Odin once swore it, on the ring. He refuses the condition, and Sigrid, not heeding his appeal, expresses her contempt of "the Southland God," and protests her constancy to the "Norland Gods." At this King Olaf's anger rises, and he strikes her cheek with his gauntlet. King Olaf is warned to fly, and the scene closes with the queen vowing vengeance on the retreating figure.

*Attention is commanded by the principal bard for the recital of the story of Thyri—the slighted choice of the Wendland King—and her flight to the North.*

## THYRI.

In a charming ballad, the minstrels sing of Thyri, the sister of Svend, the Danish king, fleeing away from King Burislaf of Wendland, to whom she had been betrothed for the short space of eight days. She comes to King Olaf's court, and Olaf eventually marries her.

After the ballad, two singers advance to represent King Olaf and the beautiful Thyri, his wife. Thyri laments the loss of her lands, which King Burislaf has possession of, and deplores her dowerless condition. Olaf, fresh from the delights of a fair morning in early spring, comes before her with a love offering of Angelicas, but with such thoughts rankling in her mind, the sweet smelling herb holds no charm for Thyri. Her mood leads her to taunt Olaf into consenting to rescue her domains from King Burislaf, upon which, having effected her purpose, she once more smiles on her lord.

*The bards join in reciting how Queen Sigrid becomes the bride of King Svend, the Dane— a union which portends evil for King Olaf—and relate how she cajoles the Danish king into setting forth to wreak vengeance on Olaf.*

## THE DEATH OF OLAF.

Full chorus of Skalds, in which are described the putting to sea of Olaf's warships to meet those of the Danes, and the contact of the opposing forces. Vividly portrayed are the deadly combat and the defeat of Olaf, who, ever foremost in the fray, is surrounded and outnumbered, and so perishes in the flood.

## EPILOGUE.

*The bard-chief finally pictures Astrid, the mother of Olaf, in the convent of Drontheim, kneeling at midnight, and listening to the voice of one speaking in the darkness without.*

The voice which Astrid heard, purports to be that of Saint John taking up the challenge in response to the entreaty of the departed spirit of Olaf.

The saga-men, echoing the words of the saint, signify the ultimate acceptance of the challenge of Thor, and the continuance of Olaf's mission, but this time, in the true Christian spirit of love, and by the power of the Great Spirit Divine, which comes "not as a vulture, but as a dove."

A. S. Burrows.

----

The Recitatives serve to prompt the narration of the Story; so, to emphasise their function and significance, the portions representing them in the above synopsis are printed in *Italics*.

----

(*From a Concert Programme of the Sheffield Musical Union.*)

# CONTENTS.

# SCENES FROM THE SAGA OF KING OLAF.

## INTRODUCTION.

Soli and Chorus.—"THERE IS A WONDROUS BOOK."

Andante.

Edward Elgar, Op. 30.

8247.

2

8247.

Skald.                                                                                    And

Skald,                                          *f*                    *dim.*              *p*        And

day,          Le - gends that    once were told or sung  By wand'ring Sa · ga · man;   And
*cres.*                                                   *dim.*

Le-gends   that once were told or   sung              By        Sa · ga · man   or
*cres.*                                                   *dim.*                    *p*

Le     ·     gends     that    once  were  told or sung By wand'ring Sa · ga · man  or
*cres.*                                                   *dim.*                    *p*

land,      Le-gends that        were     sung              By        Sa · ga · man   or
*cres.*                                                   *dim.*                    *p*

Le   ·   gends   that       once    were   sung   by    Sa · ga · man   or
*cres.*                                                   *dim.*                    *p*

*cres.*                      *f*                *dim.*        *p*

C *poco allargando.*                              *cres.*                    *f*
he who looks may find therein  The  sto · ry    that we  now      be · gin.
*poco allargando.*                               *cres.*
he who looks may find therein  The  sto · ry    that we  now      be · gin.
*poco allargando.*                               *cres.*                    *f*
he who looks may find therein  The  sto · ry    that we  now ..   be · gin.

C *pp*                                                    *ff*
Skald ;                                        Heims · kring · la

*pp*                                                     *ff*
Skald ;                                        Heims · kring · la ..

*pp*                                                     *ff*
Skald ;    ·  ·                                Heims · kring · la

*pp*                                                     *ff*
Skald ;                                        Heims · kring · la

C                                                        *8va*

*pp*              *cres. molto.*                                    *ff*

*Ped.*

**No. 1.**   RECITATIVE (BASS).—"SUMMON NOW THE GOD OF THUNDER."

B *Poco meno mosso.*

hea-vens a - sun - der, ...

Sing, sing, sing ... the

words of might - y, might - y

Thor, Chal - leng - ing the world to war. ...

*Attacca No. 2*

# THE CHALLENGE OF THOR.

### Chorus.—"I AM THE GOD THOR."

hurl it and hurl it a - far off!

hurl it, and hurl it a - far off!

And hurl it a - far off!

And hurl it a - far off!

This is .. my gir - dle, When-ev - er I brace it, Strength is re -

This is my . gir - dle, When - ev - er I

This is my ..

doub - - - led, is re - doub - led, strength, strength is re -

brace it, . . strength, strength is re -

gir - dle, When-ev-er I brace it, Strength is re - doub - led, strength, strength is re -

This is my .. gir - - - dle, strength, strength is re -

11

12

- son. Is but my red beard Blown by the night-wind, Af-tright-ing the

Is but my red beard Blown by the night-wind, Af-fright-ing the na

- son, Is but my red beard Blown by the night-wind, Af-fright-ing the

na - tions!

- tions! The

na - tions! Jove is my bro - ther,

Jove is my bro - ther; Mine eyes are the light-ning; Jove is my

14

Thus sin-gle-hand-ed Un-to the com-bat, Gaunt-let or Gos-pel.

Thus sin-gle-hand-ed Un-to the com-bat, Gaunt-let or Gos-pel,

Thus sin-gle-hand-ed Un-to the com-bat, Gaunt-let or Gos-pel,

Thus sin-gle-hand-ed Un-to the com-bat, Gaunt-let or Gos-pel,

Here I de-fy thee!

Here I de-fy thee!

Here I de-fy thee!

Here I de-fy thee!

# KING OLAF'S RETURN.

8247.

nev - er yet . . had seen One so beau - ti - ful of

mien, When in arms complete-ly fur-nished, Har-ness gold in -

laid . . and burnished, Man - tle like a flame . . of

fire, One so roy - al in . . at - tire, Man - tle like a flame, a

flame of fire. Thus came

26

8247.

27

*No. 4.*     RECIT. (BASS).—" TELL HOW OLAF BORE THE CROSS."

8247.

# THE CONVERSION.

No. 5. SOLI (TENOR AND BASS) AND CHORUS.—"KING OLAF'S PROWS AT NIDAROS."

bow - - men Lay a - round the shrine of Thor.

bow - - men Lay a - round the shrine of Thor.

bow - - men Lay a - round the shrine of Thor.

bow - - men Lay a - round the shrine of Thor.

Round the state - ly fane . . . . . at Mæ - rin, King

Round the state - ly fane . . . . at Mæ - rin, King

Round the state - ly fane . . . . at Mæ - rin, King

Round the state - ly fane . . at Mæ - rin, King

O - laf's house - carles lay, And

O - laf's house - carles lay, And

O - laf's house - carles lay, And

O - laf's house - carles lay, . . . . . . . And

watch'd the men of Drontheim Ga-ther at break of day.

watch'd the men of Drontheim Ga-ther at break of day.

watch'd the men of Drontheim Ga-ther at break of day.

watch'd the men of Drontheim Ga-ther at break of day.

C *Poco più mosso.*

Clad in mail they came, and .. sword ei,

C *Poco più mosso.* ♩. = 92.

*pp quasi alla marcia.*

Clad in mail they came, and

Cors-let and buck-ler ring,

8247.

sword - ed, As they throng be - hind the I - ron - beard, Who

throng be - hind the I - ron - beard, the I - ron -

throng be - hind,

as they throng be - hind the I - ron

leads them, who leads them to the King,

beard, . . Who leads them to . . the King, leads . . them

Corslet and buck-ler ring, . . . . I - ron - beard, I-ron-beard

- beard, . . I - ron beard, I-ron-beard

I - ron - beard, I-ron-beard

to the King, leads them to the King, I - ron - beard, I-ron-beard

leads them to the King, I - ron - beard, I-ron-beard

leads them to the King, . . I - ron - beard, I - ron - beard

dim.
leads them to the King, . to the King, . . to the
leads them to the King, I - ron - beard leads them to . the
leads them to the King, . . I - ron - beard leads
leads them to the King, I - ron - beard leads them to the
King.
King.
them to . . the King,
King, to the King, . .
pp
Cors-let and buck-ler ring.
Cors-let and buck - ler ring.
The
p

84

8247.

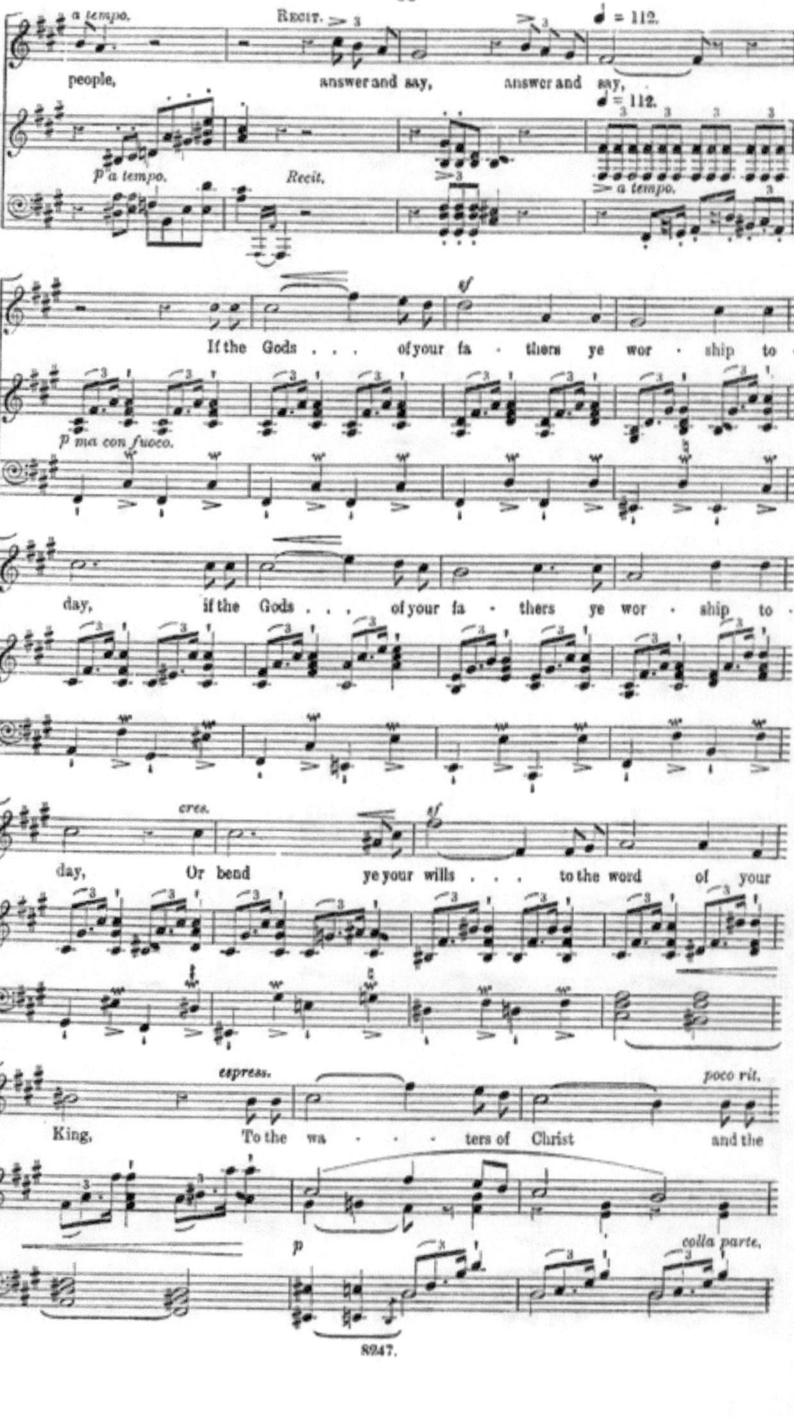
a tempo.
Recit.
♩ = 112.
people,
answer and say,
answer and say,
♩ = 112.
p a tempo.
Recit.
a tempo.
If the Gods . . . of your fa - thers ye wor - ship to -
sf
p ma con fuoco.
day,
if the Gods . . . of your fa - thers ye wor - ship to -
cres.
sf
day, Or bend ye your wills . . . to the word of your
espress.
poco rit.
King, To the wa - - - ters of Christ and the
p
colla parte.

*dim.*        *a tempo.*

cross . . that I bring, . . . the wa . ters of

*colla parte.*        *a tempo.*

Christ    and    the    cross    that    I    bring?

*accel.*      *ff*

An . swer and say.

*colla parte.*    *a tempo.*

*ten.*

IRONBEARD. RECIT. (BASS.)

By my beard call'd of I . ron,        O King! shalt thou

*Recit.* **p**      *trem.*      *sfp*

*allargando.*

know, . . . . . In the name . . of thy peo . ple, I

*sfp*      *colla parte.*    *cres.*

8247.

Who feed on the flesh and the life-blood of man?

Gods' ban,      Who

Gods' ban,      Who

*allargando.*     *a tempo.*

feed on the flesh and the life-blood of man?.. No!..

feed on the flesh and the life-blood of man?.. No!..

No!..     No!

No!..     No!

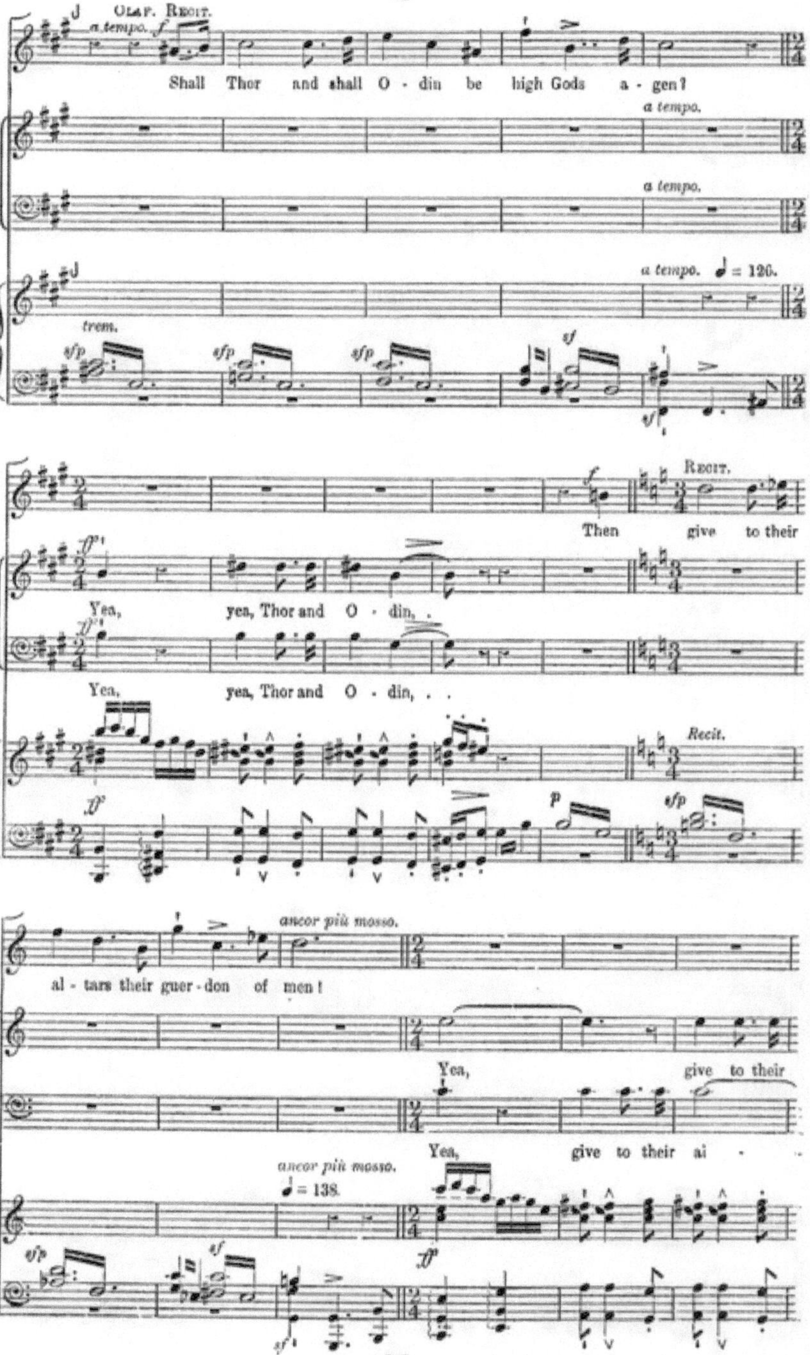

Shall Thor and shall O - din be high Gods a - gen?

Yea, yea, Thor and O - din, . .

Then give to their

al - tars their guer - don of men!

Yea, give to their

Yea, give to their ai - -

44

8247.

-gainst the gold - en im - age Flash'd O - laf's axe on high; As

-gainst the gold - en im - age Flash'd O - laf's axe on high;

Flash'd, flash'd O - laf's axe on

Flash'd O - laf's axe on

falls, as falls a berg in spring - time, Far

As falls, as falls a berg in spring time,

high; as falls a berg in spring time, Far

high; As falls, As falls a berg in spring - time,

Ped. ✱ Ped. ✱ Ped. ✱ Ped. ✱

shi - ver'd on the floe,

Shi - ver'd on the floe, The

shi - ver'd on the floe,

Shi - ver'd on the floe, The

strepitoso.

Ped. 8247. ✱

*poco allargando.*

IRONBEARD.
*Moderato.*

All - Fa - ther, I come! true to

*Moderato.* ♩ = ♩ *of preceding movement.*

hou - our and troth, To the faith of my fa - thers, and

*Lento.* ♩ = ♩ *of preceding movement.*

O - din the Goth. Oh, wide should the doors .. of Val -

*molto cantabile.*

hal - la un - roll, .. For a he - ro, a he - ro who gives,

Norseman! per - chance it may be, That thy Peace-God shall rule .. .. o'er the Nor - land - er free ; But with axe in his hand, .. with sword up - on thigh, And his face to his slay - er doth I - ron - beard die!

come be you the seal, Pass . . the Gods of the Goth

- land ; your serf-dom shall cease ; For the sac-ri-fice bloody, I of-fer you

peace, The peace . . . of the Chris - tian oh

join . . in the prayer . . That swells . . to the Lord of the earth and the air.

CHORUS.

Re - ceive us,

Re - ceive us,

Re - ceive us,

Re - ceive us,

King; we kneel to .. Him    Who fell'd by thee the ..

King; we kneel to .. Him    . Who fell'd by thee the ..

King; we kneel to .. Him    . Who fell'd by thee the ..

King; we kneel to .. Him    . Who fell'd by thee the ..

*Ped.*    *

War - God grim;    Wa - ter bring our brows to lave, And on our

War - God grim; . .    Wa - ter bring our brows to lave,.. And on our

War - God grim;    Wa - ter bring our brows to lave,.. And on our

War - God grim;    Wa - ter bring our brows to lave,.. And on our

*dim.*

*Ped.*    *    *Ped.*    *

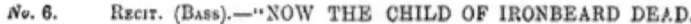

**No. 6.** RECIT. (BASS).—"NOW THE CHILD OF IRONBEARD DEAD.

Now the child of I-ron-beard dead, Fair Gu-drun doth O-laf wed, Hop-ing thus his wer-gild pay-ing, To redeem him from the slay-ing.

*Attacca No. 7*

8247

# GUDRUN.

**No. 7.** Soli (Soprano and Tenor) and Chorus.—"ON KING OLAF'S BRIDAL NIGHT.

tide of .. dreams.    At the fa - tal midnight

hour,    When all e - vil things    have pow - er,    In the

glim -mer of the moon    Stands .. Gu - drun.    Close .. against her

heav - ing breast,    Something in her hand is    pressed ; . .    Like an

fall - ing on the floor : .. 'Tis no ... thing

more ; ..

Olaf.

Ah ! For-ests have ears, and fields have eyes ;

'Tis .. the bod - kin, 'tis no - thing more ; It woke me .. fall ing

Of - ten treach - er - y lurk - ing lies Un-der - neath the .. fair - est

on ... the floor, it woke me .. fall-ing on the

hair ! Gu - drun, .. be - ware, Gu -

And for ev-er sun-dered ride      Bridegroom and

And for ev-er sun-dered ride      Bridegroom and

Bridegroom and

Bridegroom and

bride! ..

bride! ..

bride!

bride! ..

No. 8.   RECIT. (BASS).—"HOW THE WRAITH OF ODIN OLD."

8247.

# THE WRAITH OF ODIN.

CHORUS (BALLAD).—"THE GUESTS WERE LOUD."*

5247

head the smok - y raft - ers rang.

head .. the smok - y raft - ers rang.

(Dead rides Sir Mor - ten of

Fo - gel - sang.)

(Dead rides Sir Mor - ten of Fo - gel - sang.)

The door swung wide,

The door swung wide,

con Ped.

8247.

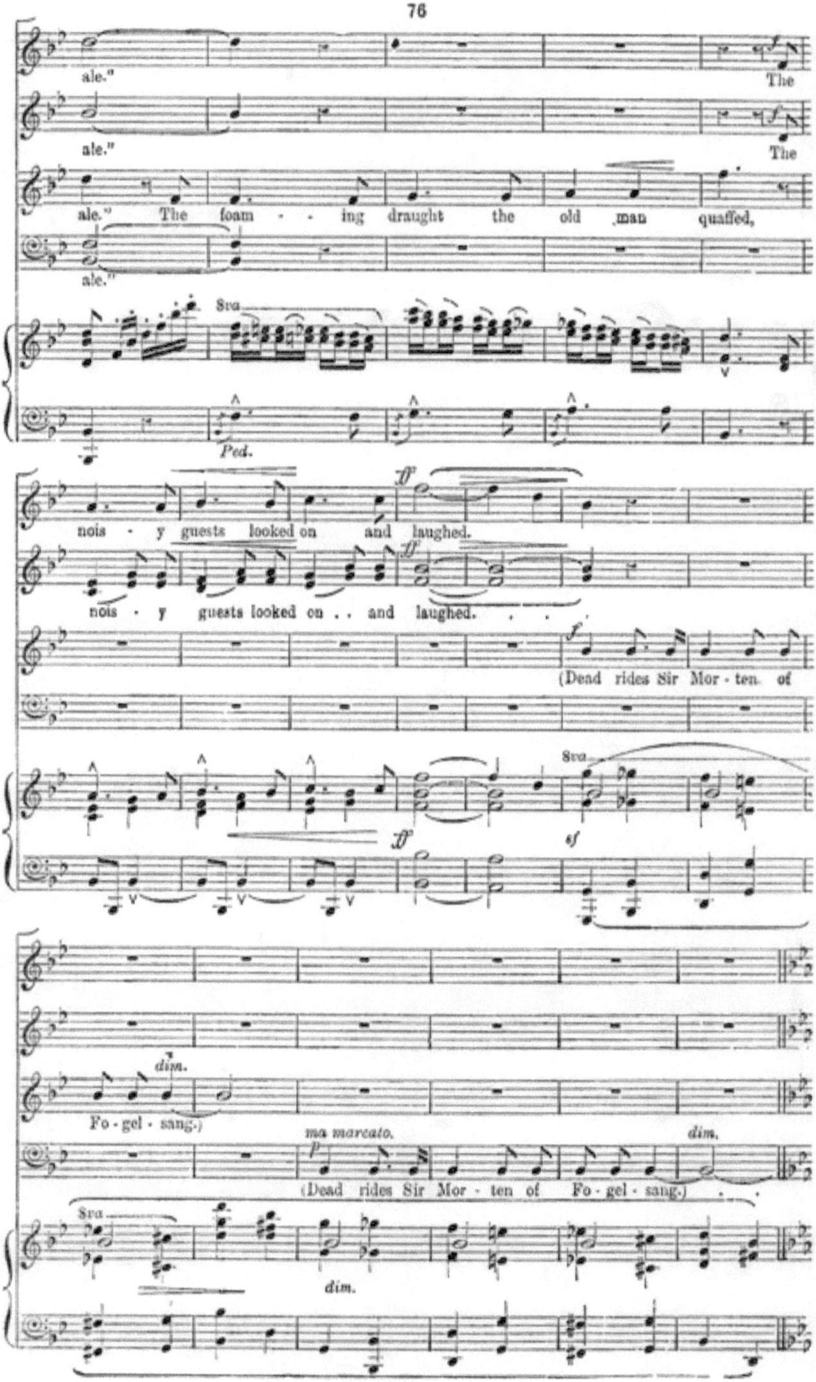
ale."
The
ale."
The
ale." The foam - - ing draught the old man quaffed,
ale."
8va
Ped.
nois - y guests looked on and laughed.
nois - y guests looked on . . and laughed. . .
(Dead rides Sir Mor - ten of
8va
sf
dim.
Fo - gel - sang.)
ma marcato.
dim.
(Dead rides Sir Mor - ten of Fo - gel - sang.)
8va
dim.

Then slept the King,

Then slept the King,

Then slept the King, then

slept the King,

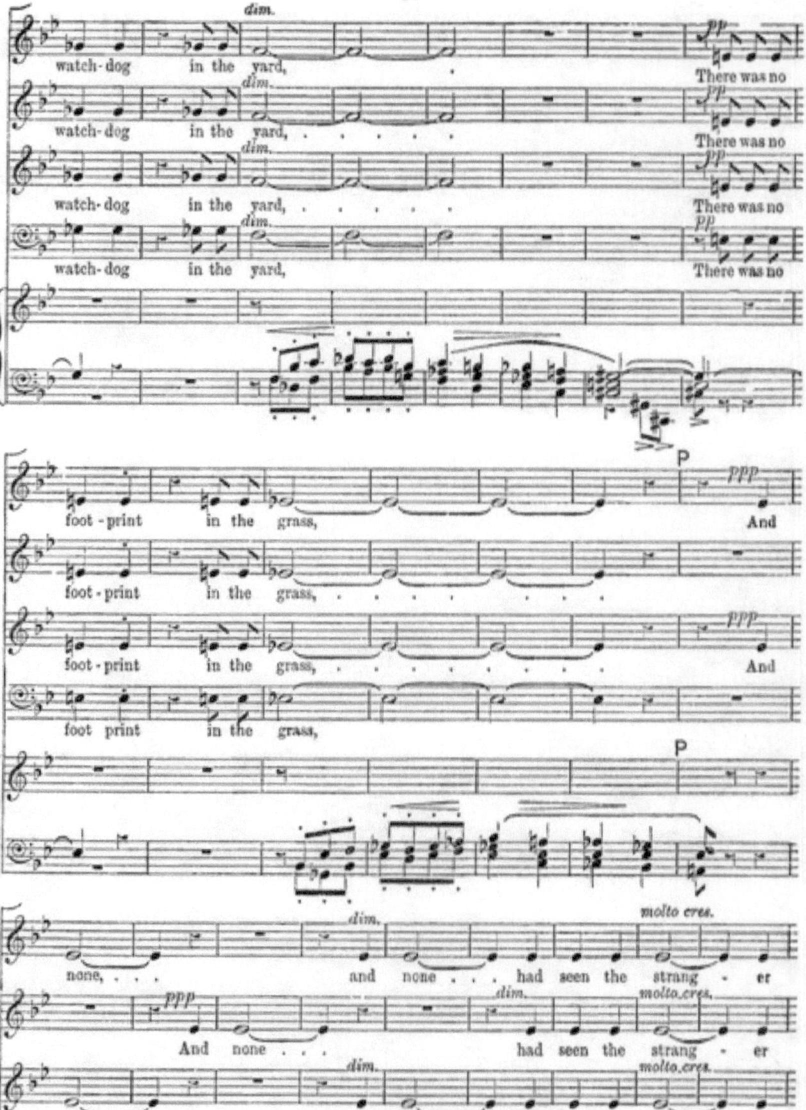
dim.
watch-dog in the yard,
pp
There was no
watch-dog in the yard,
There was no
watch-dog in the yard,
There was no
watch-dog in the yard,
There was no
P
foot-print in the grass,
ppp
And
foot-print in the grass,
foot-print in the grass,
And
foot print in the grass,
P
molto cres.
none, and none had seen the strang - er
ppp
And none had seen the strang - er
none, and none had seen the strang - er
And none had seen the strang - er
ppp
dim.
molto cres.

O - din the Great . . is dead; . . . . Sure

O - din the Great . . is dead; . . . . Sure

O - din the Great . . is dead; . . . . Sure

O - din the Great . . is dead; . . . . Sure

is the tri - umph of our . . Faith, . . . .

is the tri - umph of our Faith, . . . .

is the tri - umph of our Faith, . .

is the tri - umph of our Faith, . . .

The one - eyed strang - er was . . his wraith, . . .

The one - eyed strang - er was . . his wraith, .

The one - eyed strang - er was . . his wraith, .

The one - eyed strang - er was . . his wraith . . .

his wraith."
his wraith."
his wraith."
his wraith." . .

(Dead rides Sir Mor - ten of Fo - gel - sang.)
(Dead rides Sir Mor - ten of Fo - gel - sang, . . dead rides Sir Mor - ten of
(Dead rides Sir Mor - ten of Fo - gel - sang, . . dead rides Sir Mor - ten of
(Dead rides Sir Mor - ten of Fo - gel - sang, . . dead rides Sir Mor - ten of

Fo - gel - sang.)
Fo - gel - sang.)
Fo - gel - sang.)

Also published in Novello's Tonic Sol-fa Series, No. 1350.

No. 10   RECIT.—"SISTERS, SING YE NOW THE SONG."

Attacca No. 11

# SIGRID.

No. 11.    Soli (Soprano and Tenor) and Chorus.—"SIGRID SITS IN HER HIGH ABODE."

all, but the crest .. of .. O - laf is .. o - ver them

all, but the crest of O - laf is o - ver them

all, but the crest .. of O - laf is o - ver them

all .. And the peace-strings bind his sword ; ..

all. And the peace - strings bind . his sword ; ..

all. .. See, he a -

The Nor - ro-way king, .. with the gold - en hair.

Queen Si - grid greet thy lord.

dim.

- lights and mounts .. the stair, . Queen Si - grid greet,

dim.

pp

D.

greet .. thy lord.

G ♩ = 76.    OLAF.    mf    cres.

Si - grid, hail! .. Si - grid, hail! with

roy - al hand Knit to thee, Nor - roway's king .. and land,    And the

ring .. of La - de up - on .. thy knee, We will change, change to a

con Ped.    6247.

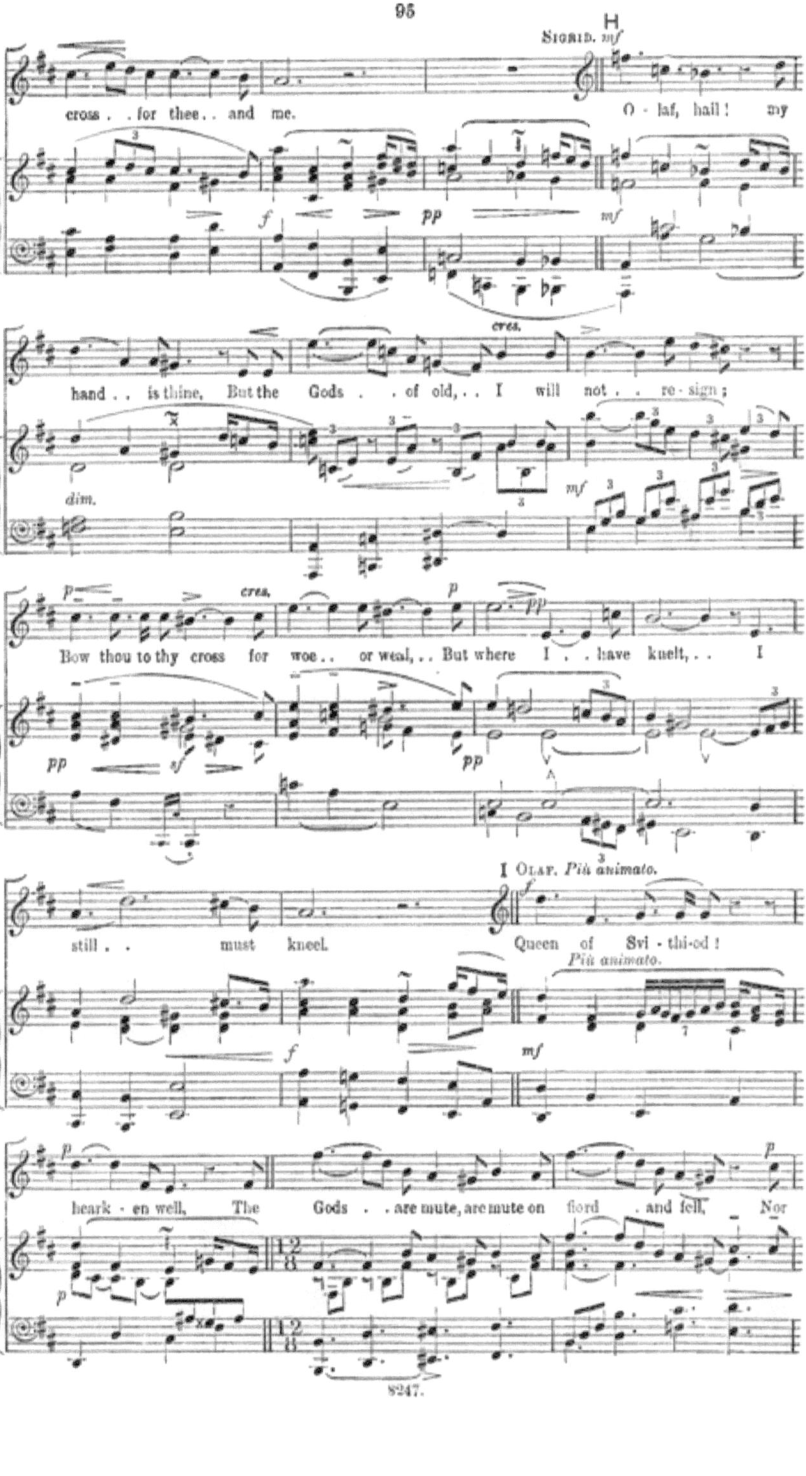

SIGRID. *mf*

cross .. for thee .. and me.

O - laf, hail! my

hand .. is thine, But the Gods .. of old, .. I will not .. re-sign;

*cres.*

*dim.*

*mf*

Bow thou to thy cross for woe .. or weal, .. But where I .. have knelt, .. I

*p* *cres.* *p*

*pp* *sf* *pp*

still .. must kneel.

Queen of Svi - thi-od!

OLAF. *Più animato.*

*Più animato.*

*f* *mf*

heark - en well, The Gods .. are mute, are mute on fiord .. and fell, Nor

*p*

*p*

*espress.*      *cres. accel.*

ev - er shall .. their voice .. a - gain .. Be heard, .. where Christ .. has

*pp*

ris - en to reign.

**J** SIGRID. *Più animato.*

I hear them speak ! from pole .. to pole .. The

*Più animato*

*stringendo.*

Nor - land Gods their thunder roll ! ..                 For

CHORUS. 1st & 2nd SOPRANOS.

Their   thun - - - - der roll ! ..

1st & 2nd CONTRALTOS.

Their   thun - - - - der roll ! ..

*stringendo.*

*ff*

**K** *Allegro con fuoco.* ♩ = 138.

Nor - - land, Nor - land folk .. the

*Allegro con fuoco.*

*fz p ben marcato.*

Olaf.

I will give my body and soul to God.

God.

ffz stringendo.    ffz    dim.

stringendo.

flame! . .    Ere I take    to my    heart . .    a

ffz stringendo.    p

heathen dame.    Thou hast    not beau - ty,

sf    p    sf

cres.

thou hast    not youth, .    Shall    I    buy    thy

p    sf    p

land . . . at the cost of truth.

1st & 2nd Sopranos.

King O-laf ris - - es;

1st & 2nd Contraltos.

King O-laf ris - - es;

sis-ters, say, Why does he thrust . . the queen a-way, . .

sis-ters, say, Why does he thrust . . the queen a-way,

Why dash his glove on the oak-en floor, . . And turn . . . and

Why dash his glove on the oak-en floor, . . And turn . . . and

floor; By my fa ther's head and the
soul of Thor. By the hand she
of fered, Si grid saith.
By the hand she of fered, Si grid yet

shall . . be O . . laf's death!

No. 12.  Recit. (Bass).—"HARK! SHE FLIES FROM WENDLAND FORTH."

# THYRI.

**No. 18.**     Chorus (Ballad).—"A LITTLE BIRD IN THE AIR."

And af - - ter a row- ful bride went she; week and a day, She has fled a - way and a - way, From his town by the storm - - - - y

8247.

she has come to King O - laf's court, . . And the town is

O - laf,

she has come to King O - laf's court, . . And the town is

O - laf,

all in dis - may,

She has come to King O - laf's court, And the

all . in dis - may, She has come to King O - laf's

And the gos-sips re - port, . . She has come to King

town is all in dis - may, The gos-sips re - port, . .

court,

pp subito, dolcissimo.

8247

whispered King O-laf has seen, ... Has talked with the beau-ti-ful Queen; ..

whispered King O-laf has seen, ... Has talked with the beau-ti-ful Queen; ..

o - ther.

And they won - der, won-der how it will end; . .

. . And they won - der, won-der how it will end; . . .

For sure-ly, if here she re-main, ... It is war with King

For sure-ly, if here she re-main, ... It is war with King

war, it is war with King Svend the Dane, And King Bu - ris

War with King Svend the Dane, And King Bu - ris

It is war with King Svend the Dane, And King Bu - ris -

It is war, war, it is war,

dim.

- laf, King Bu - ris - laf the Vend!

dim.

- laf, King Bu - ris - laf the Vend!

dim.

laf, King Bu - ris - laf! war, war, . . it is

war, it is war. war, . . it is

dim.

It is published

O, great - est won - der of all! It is

war.

war.

it roars . . . . . . . . . like a

like a flame, it roars, . The

like a flame, The

The

flame, . . . the King— . Has wed - ded her with his

King— yes, O - laf the King— . Has wed - ded her with his

King— yes, O - laf the King— . . Has wed - ded her with his

King— yes, O - laf the King— . . . Has wed - ded her with his

Ped. ✳ Ped. 8247. ✳ Ped.

No. 14.   DUET (SOPRANO AND TENOR).—"THE GRAY LAND BREAKS TO
LIVELY GREEN."

*Allargando.*   *f a tempo.*

The gray land breaks to live - ly green Be - spang ... led

*colla voce.*   *f a tempo.*

all .. with flow'rs.

*f*   *sf*

But what care I, ..

*pp*

what care I for flow'r on sward, Or burst - ing bud .. on tree! ..

*dolce.*

Ped.  * Ped.  *

My lands restored from Wend-land's lord Were bet - ter cheer to me, ...

Ped.  * Ped.  * Ped.  *     8247.

*a tempo.*

Earliest boon of Spring - time, Sign of snow de - part - - ing; In their welcome fra - - grance

*a tempo.* ♩ = 56.    *cres.*

*poco rit.*    *p*    J ♩ = 72.

Bathe thy snowy brow, bathe thy snow - y brow.

*colla parte.*    ♩ = 72.    *a tempo.*

THYRI. *dolce.*

Sweet are thy words, but oh! me-seems A sweet-er gift . would be..

*a tempo.* ♩ = 80.

*accel.*    *cres.*    *dim.*

The boon that haunts Queen Thy - ri's dreams,

*pp*    *dolce.*

*cres.*    K    *ff*

Her dow - ry o - ver sea. . Wide spread they from the Wendland

*cres.*

shore, And rich with fruit and flower, The

land I weep for ev - er - more, O! give me back my dow - er, .. O! give ..

me back my dow'r.

Fear not, doubt not, weep not,

As a Queen tri - um - phant, To the

1

OLAF. As a Queen tri-um-phant, To the hap--py

For thy love I gird me, And the lands of Thy-ri Shall I win for

sun-light I lift once more mine eyes; For my love, O gird thee,

prize, . . For thy love I gird me,.. And .. the lands .. of

And .. my lands, . . my dow-ry, Win a-gain for

Thy-ri Shall I win . a-gain, . a-gain . for

pro - mise . . . Passed from lord . . . to

pro - mise . . . Passed from lord . . . to

8ves ad lib.

la - dy, . . . Warm with words . . of lov . . .

la - dy, . . . Warm with words . . of lov . . .

dim.

- ing, Lifts the heart, . . lifts . the heart . from

- ing, Lifts the heart, lifts . the heart from

dim.

dim. p poco a poco tranquillo.

dim.

R Lento. ♩ = 108.

thrall. express.

dim. pp

thrall. Warm . . . with words of . .

R Lento.

pp ten.

CHORAL RECIT.—"AFTER QUEEN GUNHILD'S DEATH."

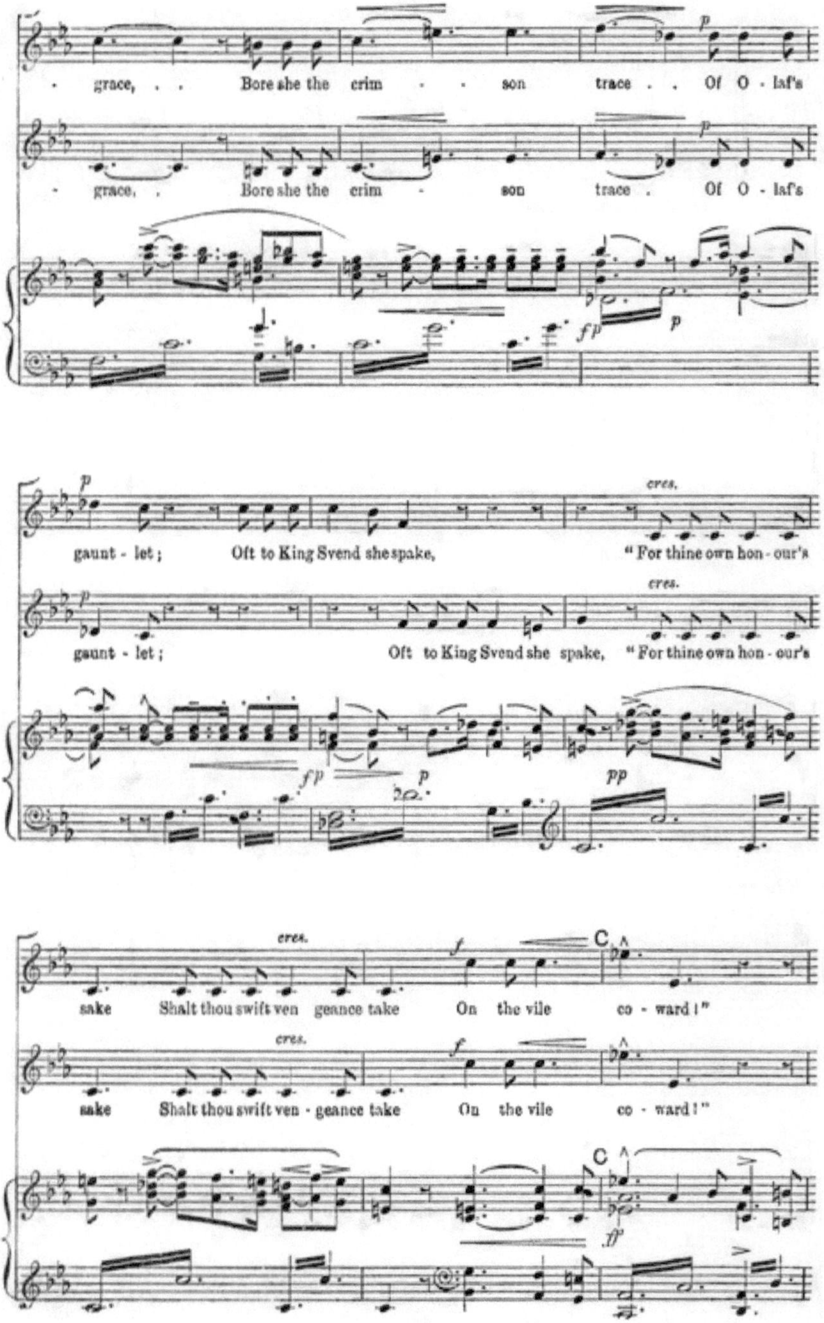

grace, . . . Bore she the crim - - son trace . . Of O - laf's

grace, . Bore she the crim - son trace . Of O - laf's

gaunt - let; Oft to King Svend she spake, "For thine own hon - our's

gaunt - let; Oft to King Svend she spake, "For thine own hon - our's

sake Shalt thou swift ven - geance take On the vile co - ward!"

sake Shalt thou swift ven - geance take On the vile co - ward!"

And to a - venge his bride, Sooth - ing her wound - ed pride,

And to a - venge his bride, Sooth - ing her wound - ed pride,

O - - ver the wa - ters, the wa - ters wide,

O - - ver the wa - ters, the wa - ters wide,

King

King

O - - laf . . . sought he, O - ver the

O - - laf . sought he, O - ver the

O - ver the

O - ver the

8247.

wa-ters wide . . King O - laf     sought he.

wa-ters wide . . King O - laf     sought he.

wa-ters wide . . King O - laf     sought he.

wa-ters wide . . King O - laf     sought he.

# THE DEATH OF OLAF.

**No. 16.**    CHORUS.—"KING OLAF'S DRAGONS TAKE THE SEA."

8247.

drives them, drives them fast,

drives them, drives them fast,

The shields dip deep up-on the lee, . . .

The shields dip deep up-on the lee, . . .

The shields dip deep up-on the lee, . . .

The white sails . . strain on ev-'ry mast . . . . .

The white sails . . strain on ev-'ry mast.

. . . The white sails . . strain on ev-'ry mast.

see far stretch'd on ei-ther side . . The Dan - ish ships and

see far stretch'd on ei-ther side . . The Dan - ish ships and

see far stretch'd on ei-ther side . . The Dan - ish ships and

see far stretch'd on ei-ther side . . The Dan - ish ships and

Svith - iod's ride.

Svith - iod's ride.

Svith - iod's ride.

Svith - iod's ride.

D *Vivace.*

D *Vivace.* ♩. = 120.

High on his deck King O - laf stands,

High on his deck King O - laf stands, With

High on his deck With war - axe grasped in both his
O - laf stands,

High on his deck King O - laf stands, With

With helm of gold And

helm, . . with helm . . of gold and jer - kin red, And

hands, With helm of gold And

helm, . . with helm . . of gold and jer - kin red.

fair curls blowing a - round his head.

fair curls blowing a - round . . his head.

fair curls blowing a - round . . his head. First of his fleet, he leads the van

First of his fleet, he leads the van . . .

8247.

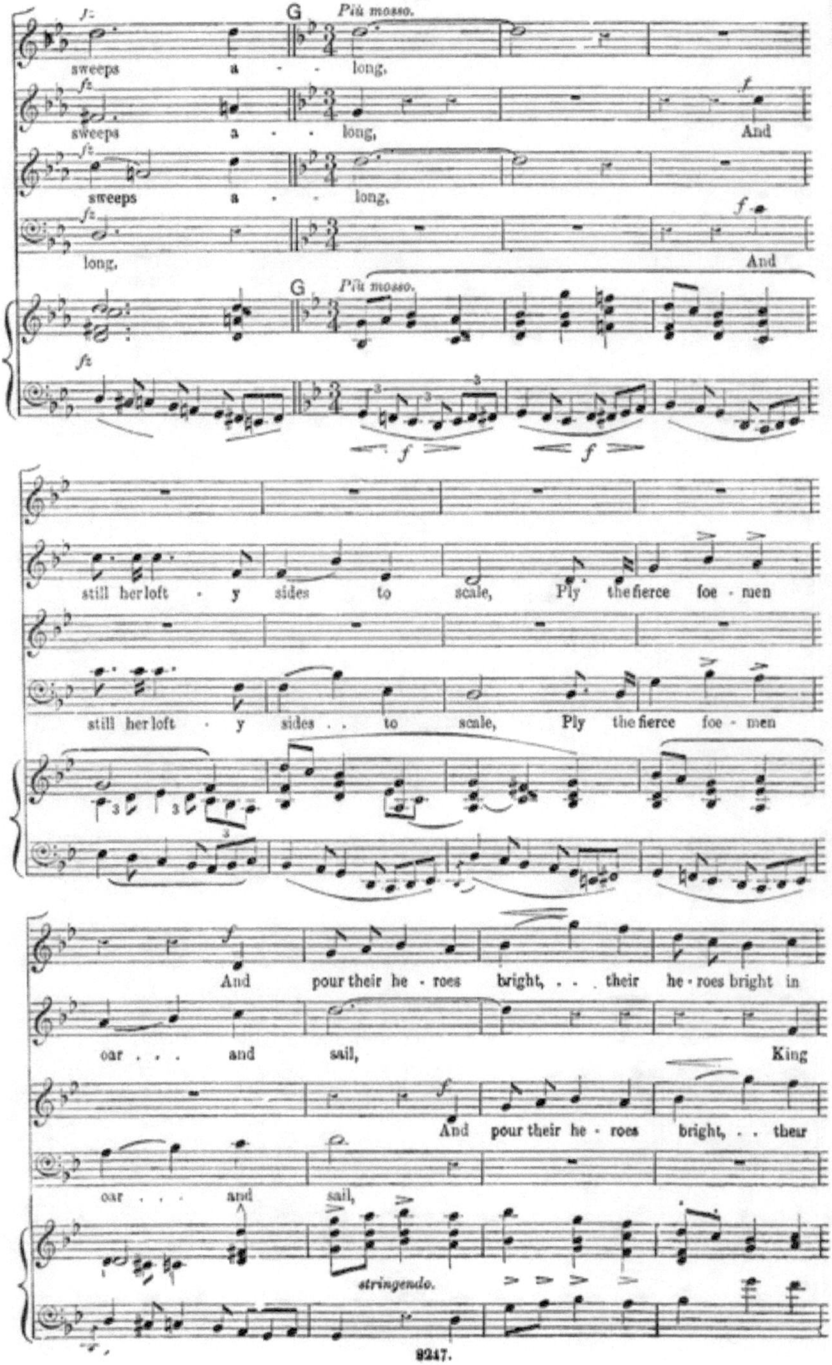

sweeps a - - long,

sweeps a - - long, And

sweeps a - - long, f

long, And

still her loft - y sides to scale, Ply the fierce foe - men

still her loft - y sides . . to scale, Ply the fierce foe - men

And pour their he - roes bright, . . . their he - roes bright in

oar . . . and sail, King

And pour their he - roes bright, . . their

oar . . . and sail,

stringendo.

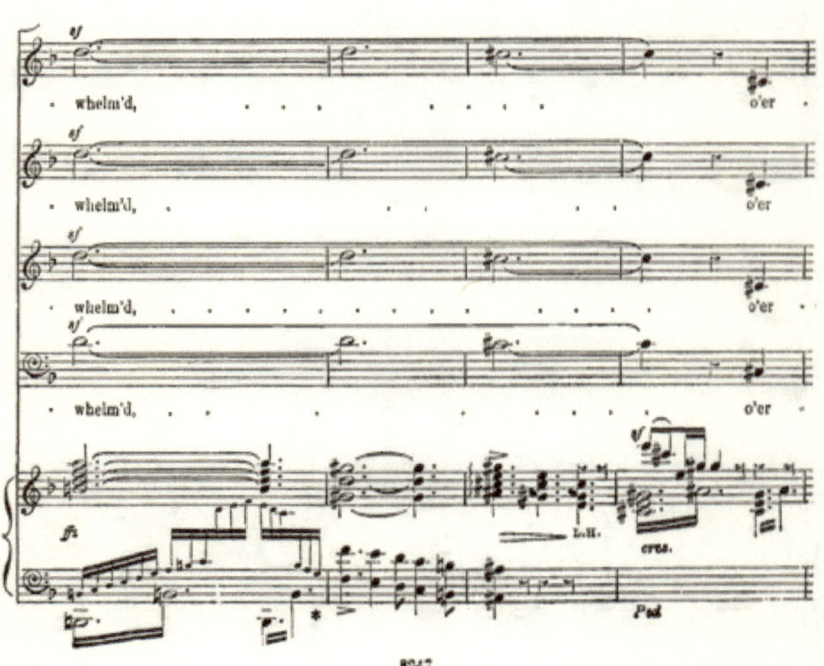

fly,

fly,

scattered pow'r - less, scarce - ly try To join once more the fray:

fly, Or . . scat - tered, scattered pow'r - less,

Or scattered power - less, scarce - ly

scarce - ly try To join once more the fray:

try To join once more the fray:

Yet still like sun - beam thro' a cloud,

Yet still like sun - beam thro' a cloud,

8ves.

8247.

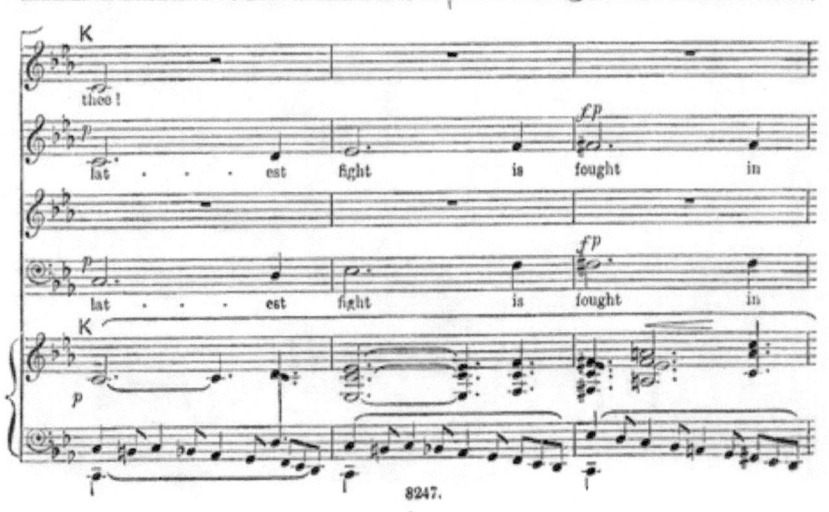

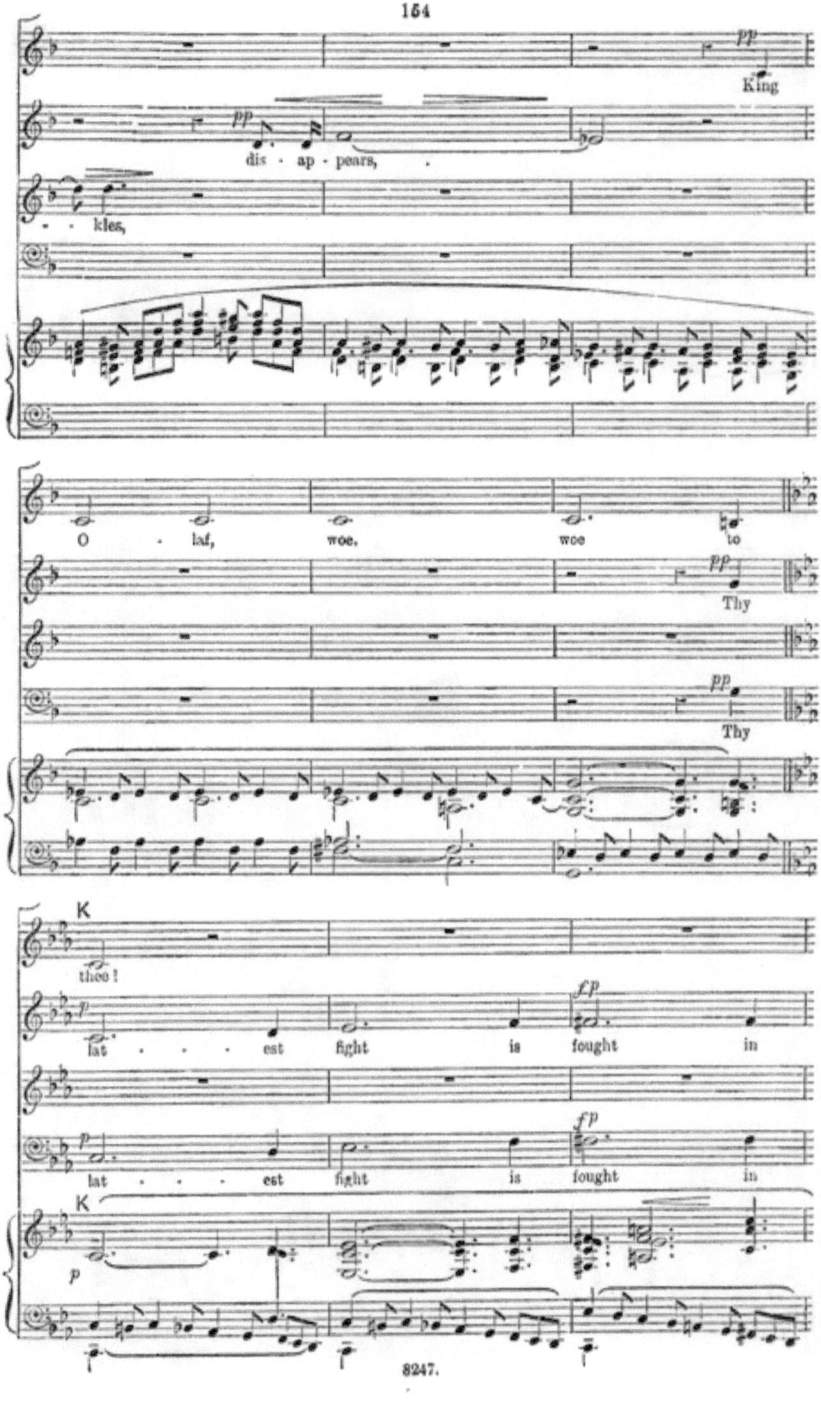
pp
King
pp
dis - ap - pears,
kles,
O - laf, woe, woe to
pp
Thy
pp
Thy
K
thee!
p
lat - - - - est fight is fought in
fp
p
lat - - - - est fight is fought in
fp
K
p

storm — — y heart hath

storm — — y heart hath

storm — y heart hath

storm — y heart hath

rest.

rest.

rest.

rest.

158

*Attacca Epilogue.*

8247.

# EPILOGUE.

**Soli and Chorus.—"IN THE CONVENT OF DRONTHEIM."**

speak - ing, With - out in the dark - ness,

B a tempo.

B

8va-

pp a tempo.

RECIT.

a tempo.

RECIT. pp

Now loud - er, now near - er, . .

Now

colla parte.

a tempo.

Più lento.

lost in the dis - tance. . .

Più lento.

ppp

Andante.

C SOLO. SOPRANO.

pp

"It is ac - cept - - ed, The

SOLO. TENOR.

pp

"It is ac - cept - - ed, The

SOLO. BASS.

pp

"It is ac - cept - - ed, The

Andante. ♩ = 84.

C

pp

F ♩ = 76. Chorus.

As tor-rents in sum-mer, Half dried in their chan-nels,

As tor-rents in sum-mer, Half dried in their chan-nels,

As tor-rents in sum-mer, Half dried in their chan-nels,

As tor-rents in sum-mer, Half dried in their chan-nels,

F ♩ = 76.

dim. Voices only.

ten. 3   ten. 3   dim.

Sud-den-ly rise, sud-den-ly rise, tho' the Sky is still cloud-less, the sky is still

ten. 3   dim.

Sud-den-ly rise, sud-den-ly rise, tho' the Sky is still cloud-less, the sky is still

Sud-den-ly rise, tho' the Sky is still cloud-less, the sky is still

dim.

Sud-den-ly rise, sud-den-ly rise, tho' the Sky is still cloud-less, the sky is still

dim.

G   pp   mf

cloud-less, For rain, . . . for rain has been

pp   mf

cloud-less, For rain, for rain has been

cres.

cloud-less, For rain, for rain has been

cloud-less,

G   p   cres.   mf

* The notes within brackets are intended for practice only.

8247.

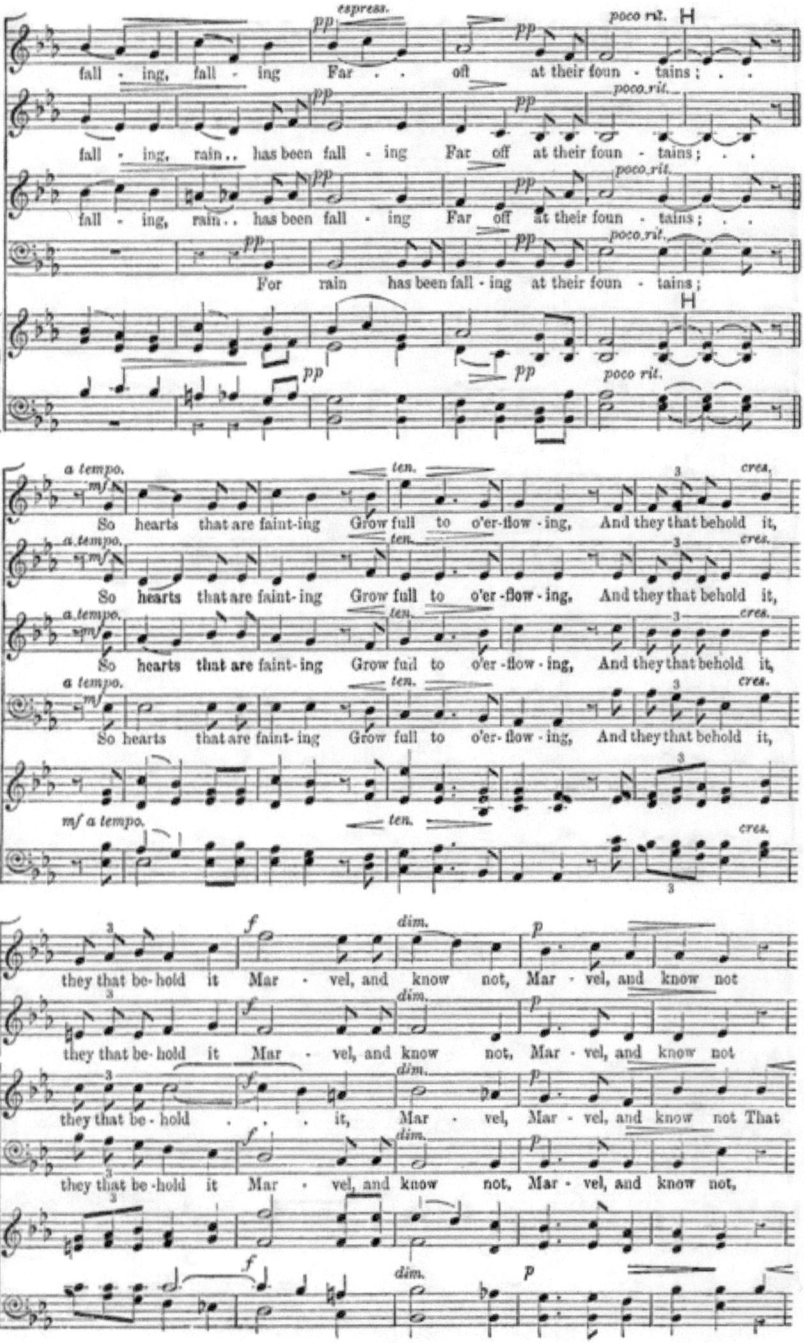
espress.
poco rit.
H
fall - ing, fall - ing Far . . oft at their foun - tains; . .
poco rit.
fall - ing, rain . . has been fall - ing Far off at their foun - tains; . .
poco rit.
fall - ing, rain . . has been fall - ing Far off at their foun - tains; . .
poco rit.
For rain has been fall - ing at their foun - tains;
poco rit.
a tempo.
ten.
cres.
So hearts that are faint-ing Grow full to o'er-flow - ing, And they that behold it,
So hearts that are faint-ing Grow full to o'er-flow - ing, And they that behold it,
So hearts that are faint-ing Grow full to o'er-flow - ing, And they that behold it,
So hearts that are faint-ing Grow full to o'er-flow - ing, And they that behold it,
mf a tempo.
dim.
they that be-hold it Mar - vel, and know not, Mar - vel, and know not
they that be-hold it Mar - vel, and know not, Mar - vel, and know not
they that be - hold . . . it, Mar - vel, Mar - vel, and know not That
they that be-hold it Mar - vel, and know not, Mar - vel, and know not,

Strong-er than steel Is the sword of the Spi-rit; Swift-er, swift-er than

love, is love, and sub - du - eth!

love, is love, and sub du - eth!

an - ger is love, and sub - du - eth!

Chorus. f = 100.

The dawn is not dis - tant, Nor is the night

The dawn is not dis - tant, Nor is the night

The dawn is not dis - tant, Nor is the night

The dawn is not dis - tant, Nor is the night

f animato. = 100.

star - less; Love is e - ter nal! God is

star - less; Love is e-ter - nal, love is e-ter - nal! God is

star - less; Love is e - ter nal! God is

star - less: Love . . . is e - ter - nal! God is

THE END

# NOVELLO'S OCTAVO EDITION OF
# ORATORIOS, CANTATAS, MASSES, &c.

## PRICE ONE SHILLING EACH.

**THOMAS ADAMS.**
CROSS OF CHRIST, THE
GOLDEN HARVEST, A
HOLY CHILD, THE
NATIVITY, THE
RAINBOW OF PEACE, THE

**THOMAS ANDERTON.**
NORMAN BARON, THE
WRECK OF THE HESPERUS, THE

**E. ASPA.**
GIPSIES, THE

**ASTORGA.**
STABAT MATER.

**BACH.**
BE NOT AFRAID. 8d.
BIDE WITH US.
CHRIST LAY IN DEATH'S DARK PRISON.
CHRISTMAS ORATORIO. PARTS 1—2.
DITTO DITTO. PARTS 3—4.
DITTO DITTO. PARTS 5—6.
COME, JESU, COME (MOTET).
COME, REDEEMER OF OUR RACE.
FROM DEPTHS OF WOE I CALL ON THEE.
GIVE THE HUNGRYMAN THY BREAD
GOD GOETH UP WITH SHOUTING.
GOD SO LOVED THE WORLD.
GOD'S TIME IS THE BEST.
HOW BRIGHTLY SHINES YON STAR OF MORN.
IF THOU BUT SUFFEREST GOD TO GUIDE THEE.
JESU, PRICELESS TREASURE (MOTET).
JESUS, NOW WILL WE PRAISE THEE.
JESUS SLEEPS, WHAT HOPE REMAINETH.
LET SONGS OF REJOICING BE RAISED.
LORD IS A SUN AND SHIELD, THE
LORD IS MY SHEPHERD, THE
LORD, REBUKE ME NOT.
MAGNIFICAT IN D.
MY SPIRIT WAS IN HEAVINESS.
NOW SHALL THE GRACE. 6d.
JESU CHRIST, THOU PRINCE OF PEACE.
O LIGHT EVERLASTING
PRAISE THE LORD FOR ALL HIS MERCIES.
TEACH ME, LORD, MY DAYS TO NUMBER.
PRAISE OUR GOD WHO REIGNS IN HEAVEN.
PRAISE THOU THE LORD, JERUSALEM.
SING YE TO THE LORD (MOTET).
SLEEPERS, AWAKE.
SAGES OF SHEBA, THE
SPIRIT ALSO HELPETH US, THE (MOTET).
STRONGHOLD SURE, A
THERE IS NAUGHT OF SOUNDNESS IN ALL MY BODY.
THOU GUIDE OF ISRAEL.
WAILING, CRYING, MOURNING.
WATCH YE, PRAY YE.
WHEN WILL GOD RECALL MY SPIRIT.
REBEKAH.

**J. BARNBY.**
REBEKAH.

**M. BARTON.**
MASS, IN A (UNACCOMPANIED).

**BEETHOVEN.**
CHORAL FANTASIA (OP. 80).
ENGEDI (OP. 85).
MASS, IN C (LATIN WORDS) (OP. 86).
MASS, IN C (OP. 86).
MOUNT OF OLIVES (OP. 85).

**WILFRED BENDALL.**
SONG DANCES (FEMALE VOICES).

**KAREL BENDL.**
WATER SPRITE'S REVENGE (FEMALE VOICES).

**G. J. BENNETT.**
EASTER HYMN (ON THE MORN OF EASTER DAY).

**W. STERNDALE BENNETT.**
EXHIBITION ODE, 1862.
† MAY QUEEN, THE
† WOMAN OF SAMARIA, THE

**G. R. BETJEMANN.**
THE SONG OF THE WESTERN MEN.

**HUGH BLAIR.**
HARVEST-TIDE.

**J. BRAHMS.**
† REQUIEM (OP. 45).
SONG OF DESTINY, A (OP. 54)
† RHAPSODY (OP. 53). 8d.

**J. B. van BREE.**
† ST. CECILIA'S DAY.

**A. H. BREWER.**
O PRAISE THE LORD.
SONG OF EDEN, A

**J. F. BRIDGE.**
HYMN TO THE CREATOR.
† INCHCAPE ROCK, THE
† LORD'S PRAYER, THE
† ROCK OF AGES.

**CARISSIMI.**
* JEPHTHAH.

**CHERUBINI.**
* REQUIEM MASS, IN C MINOR.
THIRD MASS, IN A (CORONATION).
FOURTH MASS, IN C.

**G. F. COBB.**
MY SOUL TRULY WAITETH.

**M. COSTA.**
DREAM, THE

**F. H. COWEN.**
† HE GIVETH HIS BELOVED SLEEP.

**B. J. DALE.**
BEFORE THE PALING OF THE STARS.

**H. WALFORD DAVIES.**
† HERVÉ RIEL.
ODE ON TIME.

**T. F. DUNHILL.**
† TUBAL CAIN.

**EDWARD ELGAR.**
GIVE UNTO THE LORD. 8d.
† GREAT IS THE LORD. 8d.
TE DEUM AND BENEDICTUS, IN F.

**ROSALIND F. ELLICOTT.**
ELYSIUM.

**G. FERRARI.**
IMPRESSIONS (VOCAL SUITE, LADIES' VOICES).

**ROBERT FRANZ.**
PRAISE YE THE LORD (OP. 19).

**NIELS W. GADE.**
† CHRISTMAS EVE (OP. 40).
† ERL-KING'S DAUGHTER, THE (OP. 30).
† SPRING'S MESSAGE (OP. 35). 8d.
ZION (OP. 49).

**H. BALFOUR GARDINER.**
† NEWS FROM WHYDAH. 8d.

**G. GARRETT**
† HARVEST CANTATA.

**F. R. GERNSHEIM.**
SALAMIS (OP. 10) (MALE VOICES).

**HERMANN GOETZ.**
BY THE WATERS OF BABYLON (OP. 14)
NOENIA (OP. 10).

**A. M. GOODHART.**
EARL HALDAN'S DAUGHTER.

**CH. GOUNOD.**
DAUGHTERS OF JERUSALEM (UNACCOMPANIED).
DE PROFUNDIS (LATIN WORDS).
DITTO (ENGLISH WORDS).
† FAUST (SELECTION, FOR CONCERT PERFORMANCES).
* † GALLIA.
MESSE SOLENNELLE, STE. CÉCILE (LATIN WORDS).
PASSION, THE
† REDEMPTION (PART 2).
† REDEMPTION (PART 3).

**GRAUN.**
PASSION OF OUR LORD, THE (CHORUSES ONLY).

**ALAN GRAY.**
LEGEND OF THE ROCK-BUOY BELL.

**J. O. GRIMM.**
SOUL'S ASPIRATION, THE

**E. V. HALL.**
† IS IT NOTHING TO YOU. 8d.

**HANDEL.**
ACIS AND GALATEA. EDITED BY V. NOVELLO.
† DITTO. EDITED BY J. BARNBY.
CHANDOS TE DEUM.
DETTINGEN TE DEUM.
DIXIT DOMINUS.
* EXCEPT THE LORD BUILD THE HOUSE.
† ISRAEL IN EGYPT (POCKET EDITION).
† JUDAS MACCABÆUS (DITTO).
† MESSIAH (DITTO).
* NISI DOMINUS.
O COME, LET US SING.
† O PRAISE THE LORD.
ODE ON ST. CECILIA'S DAY.
PASSION OF CHRIST (ABRIDGED).
UTRECHT JUBILATE.
WAYS OF ZION, THE

**C. A. E. HARRISS.**
SANDS OF DEE, THE

**J. HARRISON.**
CHRISTMAS CANTATA.
† HARVEST CANTATA.

**HAYDN.**
† CREATION, THE (POCKET EDITION).
* FIRST MASS, IN B FLAT.
FIRST MASS, IN B FLAT (LATIN).
SECOND MASS, IN C (LATIN).
THIRD MASS (IMPERIAL). (LATIN.)
* THIRD MASS (IMPERIAL).
† TE DEUM.
SEASONS, THE, FROM :
† SPRING.
SUMMER.
AUTUMN.
WINTER.

**EDWARD HECHT.**
O MAY I JOIN THE CHOIR INVISIBLE.

**H. M. HIGGS.**
ERL KING, THE

**F. HILLER.**
ALL THEY THAT TRUST (OP. 60). 8d.
† SONG OF VICTORY, A (OP. 151).

*The Works marked * have Latin and English Words.*
*Those marked thus † may be had in the Tonic Sol-fa Notation.*

LONDON : NOVELLO AND COMPANY, LIMITED.

85/9/14.

# ORATORIOS, CANTATAS, MASSES, &c.—Continued.

## PRICE ONE SHILLING EACH.

**H. HOFMANN.**
SONG OF THE NORNS (Op. 21) (Female Voices).

**HUMMEL.**
FIRST MASS, IN B FLAT (Op. 77).
SECOND MASS, IN E FLAT (Op. 80).
THIRD MASS, IN D (Op. 111).

**H. H. HUSS.**
*† AVE MARIA (Op. 4) (Female Voices).

**A. JENSEN.**
†FEAST OF ADONIS, THE

**W. JORDAN.**
BLOW YE THE TRUMPET IN ZION.

**E. H. LEMARE.**
'TIS THE SPRING OF SOULS TO-DAY.

**LEONARDO LEO.**
DIXIT DOMINUS.

**C. HARFORD LLOYD.**
O GIVE THANKS UNTO THE LORD.
SONG OF BALDER, THE

**HAMISH MacCUNN.**
† LORD ULLIN'S DAUGHTER.
† WRECK OF THE HESPERUS, THE

**G. A. MACFARREN.**
† MAY DAY.
OUTWARD BOUND.

**A. C. MACKENZIE.**
†BRIDE, THE

**F. A. MARSHALL.**
CHORAL DANCES (Prince Sprite).

**MENDELSSOHN.**
†AS THE HART PANTS (Op. 42).
†ATHALIE (Op. 74).
* AVE MARIA (Saviour of Sinners).
   (Op. 23).
* CHRISTUS (Op. 97).
† COME, LET US SING (Op. 46).
*ELIJAH (Op. 70) (Pocket Edition).
FESTGESANG (Hymns of Praise) (Male Voices).
†       DITTO       (Arranged for S.A.T.B.).
† HEAR MY PRAYER.
† HYMN OF PRAISE (Lobgesang) (Op. 52).
* † LAUDA SION (Op. 73).
† LORD, HOW LONG (Op. 96).
† LORELEY (Op. 98).
MAN IS MORTAL (Op. 23, No. 3).
† MIDSUMMER NIGHT'S DREAM (Op. 61).
*† MOTETS, THREE (Op. 39) (Female Voices).
* NOT UNTO US (Op. 31).
SING TO THE LORD (Op. 91). 8d.
†ST. PAUL (Op. 36) (Pocket Edition).
†TO THE SONS OF ART (Op. 68) (Male Voices).
†WALPURGIS NIGHT, THE FIRST (Op. 60).
†WHEN ISRAEL OUT OF EGYPT CAME (Op. 51).

**MEYERBEER.**
91ST PSALM (Latin Words).
91ST PSALM (English Words).

**MOZART.**
* FIRST MASS.
KING THAMOS.
REQUIEM MASS (Latin).
* † REQUIEM MASS.
SEVENTH MASS (Latin).
TWELFTH MASS (Latin).
* †TWELFTH MASS.

**E. MUNDELLA.**
VICTORY OF SONG (Female Voices).

**STAFFORD NORTH.**
†IN THE MORNING.

**PALESTRINA.**
SURGE ILLUMINARE.

**H. W. PARKER.**
KOBOLDS, THE

**C. H. H. PARRY.**
† BLEST PAIR OF SIRENS.
GLORIES OF OUR BLOOD AND STATE, THE
TE DEUM LAUDAMUS (Coronation, 1911).

**PERGOLESI.**
† STABAT MATER (Female Voices).

**C. PINSUTI.**
PHANTOMS.

**JOHN POINTER.**
†SONG OF HAROLD HARFAGER, THE (Male Voices).

**E. PROUT.**
FREEDOM.
†HUNDREDTH PSALM, THE

**PURCELL.**
TE DEUM AND JUBILATE, IN D.
†TE DEUM, IN D. Edited by J. F. BRIDGE.
TE DEUM, IN D (Latin).

**ROMBERG**
HARMONY OF THE SPHERES, THE (Op. 45).
† LAY OF THE BELL, THE (Op. 25).
†TRANSIENT AND THE ETERNAL, THE (Op. 42).

**ROSSINI.**
*† STABAT MATER.

**ED. SACHS.**
KING CUPS.
WATER LILIES.

**SCHUBERT.**
MASS, IN A FLAT.
MASS, IN B FLAT (Op. 141).
MASS, IN C (Op. 48).
* MASS, IN F.
MASS, IN G.
†SONG OF MIRIAM (Op. 136).
†SONG OF THE SPIRITS OVER THE WATERS (Op. 167) (Male Voices).

**SCHUMANN.**
ADVENT HYMN, "IN LOWLY GUISE." (Op. 71).
KING'S SON, THE (Op. 116).
MANFRED (Op. 115).
MIGNON'S REQUIEM (Op. 98b).
† NEW YEAR'S SONG (Op. 144).
PILGRIMAGE OF THE ROSE, THE (Op. 112).
SONG OF THE NIGHT (Op. 108).  9d.

**H. SCHUTZ.**
PASSION OF OUR LORD, THE

**B. LUARD-SELBY.**
DYING SWAN, THE

**E. SILAS.**
MAGNIFICAT IN D (Latin).
MASS, IN C.

**H. SMART.**
SING TO THE LORD.

**ALICE MARY SMITH.**
ODE TO THE NORTH-EAST WIN
RED KING, THE (Men's Voices).
† SONG OF THE LITTLE B
TUNG, THE (Men's Voices).

**SPOHR.**
CHRISTIAN'S PRAYER, THE
† GOD, THOU ART GREAT (Op. 98)
HYMN TO ST. CECILIA (Op. 97).
† LAST JUDGMENT, THE

**D. STEPHEN.**
† LAIRD O' COCKPEN, THE

**S. STOCKER.**
SONG OF THE FATES.

**S. STOJOWSKI.**
SPRINGTIME (Op. 7).

**A. SULLIVAN**
EXHIBITION ODE.
† FESTIVAL TE DEUM.
† TE DEUM (Thanksgiving for Victo

**P. TCHAIKOVSKY.**
†NATURE AND LOVE (Female Voi

**A. GORING THOMAS.**
† SUN WORSHIPPERS, THE

**E. H. THORNE.**
BE MERCIFUL UNTO ME.

**B. TOURS.**
FESTIVAL ODE, A

**ERNEST WALKER.**
HYMN TO DIONYSUS, A
ODE TO A NIGHTINGALE.

**C. M. von WEBER.**
JUBILEE CANTATA.
* MASS, IN E FLAT.
* MASS, IN G.
PRECIOSA.
THREE SEASONS.

**S. WESLEY.**
DIXIT DOMINUS.

**S. S. WESLEY.**
O LORD, THOU ART MY GOD.
† WILDERNESS, THE  6d.

**JOHN E. WEST.**
LORD, I HAVE LOVED THE HA
TATION OF THY HOUSE.
SONG OF ZION, A

**C. LEE WILLIAMS.**
†FESTIVAL HYMN, A  8d.

**C. WOOD.**
ODE TO THE WEST WIND.

**R. T. WOODMAN.**
FALMOUTH.

**F. C. WOODS.**
†GREYPORT LEGEND, A (Male Voic

*The Works marked * have Latin and English Words.*
*Those marked thus † may be had in the Tonic Sol-fa Notation.*

London: NOVELLO AND COMPANY, Limited.

25/9/14.

www.ingramcontent.com/pod-product-compliance
Lightning Source LLC
Chambersburg PA
CBHW031109020726
47495CB00007B/2122

* 9 7 8 3 7 4 4 7 8 3 4 6 0 *